A story by Museum Piece Writings

Friendship to Forevership

BLUEROSE PUBLISHERS
India | U.K.

Copyright © Snigdha Palaparthi 2023

All rights reserved by the author. No part of this publication may be reproduced, stored in a retrieval system or transmitted in any form or by any means, electronic, mechanical, photocopying, recording or otherwise, without the prior permission of the author. Although every precaution has been taken to verify the accuracy of the information contained herein, the publisher assumes no responsibility for any errors or omissions. No liability is assumed for damages that may result from the use of the information contained within.

BlueRose Publishers takes no responsibility for any damages, losses, or liabilities that may arise from the use or misuse of the information, products, or services provided in this publication.

For permissions requests or inquiries regarding this publication, please contact:

BLUEROSE PUBLISHERS
www.BlueRoseONE.com
info@bluerosepublishers.com
+91 8882 898 898
+4407342408967

ISBN: 978-93-5819-292-6

Cover design: Shivam Sharma
Typesetting: Namrata Saini

First Edition: September 2023

About the Author...

Snigdha Palaparthi, the author, possesses a balanced blend of creativity and narration as an Architect by the day and a Writer by night. After graduation, she spent several years in the field designing and creating landscapes that harmonised functionality with aesthetics. This love for detailing along with her passion for storytelling translates naturally in the form of her *Museum Piece Writings* which are beautifully constructed, with meticulous attention to the interplay of characters, settings, and emotions.

Apart from her professional hats, in her personal life, she is a superwoman, a caring and compassionate wife, a nurturing mother and an obedient daughter whose experiences imbue her writing with authenticity and relatability. She is also a devoted movie buff and a decent singer. She draws inspiration for imaginative storytelling by observing and empathising with fellow human beings. Her stories as an amateur writer can be found on her blog @MuseumPieceWritings.

With her unique perspective and multi-faceted background, Snigdha explores themes of love, family, and the complexities of relationships in this debut novel, inviting you to witness the birth of a new voice in the literary landscape.

Author Introduction penned beautifully by Vaishnavi Ravula, blog @thoughtkettle.

Acknowledgements...

The first thanks are to my husband Rakesh, my foremost person in everything. Thanks for being the harness to me as I bungee jump into the world. Thanks for being an excellent father which gives me the courage to explore my passion with all that I have.

Thanks to my amazing and beautiful son Viraj, whose love and his pure smile push me harder every day to be a better person than I was yesterday. I promise to continue to strive every day to make him proud.

Thanks to my superstar parents who gave me this life and the ability to think and imagine. I get these vocational skills from my dad and the storytelling skills from my mom. So, whatever I am today is just half of what they are.

Thanks to my partner in crime brother Kesari, who was the first ever to see my work, encouraged me to start a blog and helped me create one. He doesn't know how much his presence makes my life more valuable.

Thanks to my wonderful best friend Vaishnavi, whose support I had throughout the entire thought process. The beginning, the middle and the end. She read, re-read, corrected, and motivated me with every single chapter of this book and inspired me to write such an amazing character like Akanksha.

Last but not the least, Thanks to everyone who said *'You write well Snigdha. Maybe you should publish your work...'* You know who you are. Your words opened new doors in my life that I never knew existed. You are the ones who pushed me to think that I can actually write a book.

Chapter-1

POV – Varna

2011

I woke up, stretching widely from my Sunday afternoon nap. I looked around and saw my parents napping on the sofa, with the TV still on. We just finished watching our all-time favourite movie *Ashta Chamma* on GeminiTV and fell asleep. I had just remembered the assignments that were due for tomorrow. I proceeded to the kitchen, craving some steaming hot filter coffee. I put milk on the stove and looked back to see my mom walking towards me.

'Oh. Did I wake you maa? I'm sorry!' I said, leaning my head on her shoulder.

'No. I was waking up anyway. You go and start your homework. I'll get you coffee.' I looked at her mouthing *Thank you* and went to my room.

I got comfortable in my study chair and switched on the computer to check my mail. I also logged into Orkut.com on another window. I stared at the hypnotizing loading wheel on the screen. The screen made a notification sound, alerting my gaze towards the Orkut chat box. I opened the chat box and my eyes went wide in surprise. The message was from an old friend from so long ago. I gasped to myself aloud *Subhash...! Wow!*

He seemed like he was excited to text me too, considering the multiple y's in his message.

S: Heyyy...!!!

V: Hey man! Is that really you...!?

S: Yeah, it's me. Kavitha Auntie's son. I hope that's who you mean...!?'

V: Hahaha Yes. I don't know any other Subhash in my life.

S: Haha. How are you Varna? What are you doing these days?

V: Bachelors of Fine Arts (B.F.A) JNAFAU, Hyderabad. What about you?

S: Gitam University, Vizag. BTech.

V: Wow. Vizag huh!? Cool.

S: Yeah, I remember how much you love the beach.

V: Yes...! Do you visit the beach often?

S: I'm here for the beach more than anything else.

V: You make it sound like you don't like the rest of it. Isn't the college great? How's your study life?'

S: Meh. Study life... just keeps going. But I love the college. I have good friends here. I get to play cricket a lot. How about you? Topping your class/college and everything as usual?

V: I don't know about that. But I'm glad that I'm following my passion. I want to become a Jewellery designer. That's why the degree in Fine Arts.

Suddenly, I realized my mom was standing beside me, looking at the screen, holding my coffee. I minimized the window and said, 'Amma...! No peeking. We talked about this remember?'

'Yeah alright... I didn't get to see anything, anyway. Who was that?'

'That... was Subhash. Kavitha Auntie's son. We connected on Orkut.'

'That's nice. Let me talk to him. How is he doing? I will ask how's Kavitha doing.'

'Maa... No! Give that to me and go!'

I took the coffee cup and pushed her away. She left the room, reminding herself that she should call her friend Kavitha and catch up. Meanwhile, the chat box was buzzing with a few unread messages from Subhash.

S: Wow. You are still the same you know. Passionate, ambitious and determined.

S: Great to hear that you found your passion. I wish I knew what I want in life.

S: Hey...There?

S: Listen I need to go out. I will text you around 9:30pm when I return. Hope to hear from you then. It was lovely catching up with you Varna.

I read the messages and felt disappointed that he had to go. I was so happy talking to him. It was a big nostalgia hit. We were inseparable best friends from the ages of 6-11 years. We spent all our free time together. We played games in the community ground after school hours. We went to the same summer camp in the holidays. We did have other friends, but we both were a lot closer to each other. We lived on the same floor of the same apartment building. We used to slip out of the home on Sunday afternoons when our parents were asleep and sat on the stairs for hours talking.

I tried to navigate through my work with half a mind. I would type a line or two and then zone out completely. This repeated for quite a while until I gave up. It was almost 7:35pm. My Dad called out for me. I went to the door and asked my dad what he wanted, peeping into the living room. He asked if I'd accompany him to the Grocery store. I looked back at the system and thought this could be a good distraction. So, I left.

I always loved these evening bike rides with my dad. We would have great conversations about life, Philosophy, Astrology, the Universe and lots of other interesting subjects. Today, for some reason I was very distracted and zoned out. It was not like I was thinking about anything or anyone in particular. My mind went out of my body and wandered all around without hinting its whereabouts, leaving me absent-minded. So much, so that I didn't realize we reached the store and my dad had already asked me to get down. My dad looked back at me and yelled,

'Hello, Madam! Where's your head at?'

I exited my trance, got off the bike, and walked straight into the store. My dad parked the vehicle and came inside catching up with me. He said,

'What are you thinking Kanna? Is it College? Homework?'

'Nah. Nothing Nanna. I'm good.'

I smiled and went along with the rest of the shopping reading him the to-buy list my mom handed to me. While I was at the billing counter giving the groceries to the cashier, my dad said,

'Hey. Let's do something crazy. After this, let's go to *Spicy Delight* and have that Manchurian fried rice that you love. What say?'

I turned slowly towards him, my eyes furrowed, as I was astonished to hear this. I guess my dad convinced himself that I was not in a great mood because of something and decided to remedy it by treating me to my favourite food. But it wasn't anything like that. I was perfectly all right but just a little distracted. Anyway, I found the attempt to be sweet on his part. My dad does things like this where he doesn't address the topic in question but does some cute gestures to clear my head. It usually works wonders for me. I would not think about whatever I'm stressing about at that moment and then when I'm back to the issue my mind is much clear and relaxed to ease me through my stress.

Even though I was not stressing about anything, I could simply go along just for my favourite Manchurian Fried rice at Spicy Delight. Just the thought of it makes my mouth water. But I thought about my mom because we didn't inform her about our little detour.

'I would love that Nanna. But I guess Maa's planning on cooking. Are you sure about this?'

'We just purchased Groceries that'll run us for an entire month. There's nothing at home right now. She's probably waiting for us to get back home with these.' he said, pointing towards the two large bags. I laughed at that comment.

'We'll order some takeaway and make a night of it. I'm sure she'd appreciate that.'

I was standing in the parking lot near our bike, while my dad was writing our address down at the counter for home delivery. He looked at me through the glass door and winked.

While we were talking and walking in the corridor reaching our flat, my mom was standing at the main door with a frown and her hands on her waist. She was upset because we didn't inform her about bringing dinner. We both stopped and looked at each other. My dad started the conversation,

'Honey... We have a surprise for you. We brought dinner from your favourite *Spicy Delight*...! So that you can have a well-deserved rest for the night from the kitchen.'

Saying that he slowly walked towards her with a broad smile on his face. She immediately cooled down and smiled at him. Their relationship always warms my heart. Theirs was a love marriage. They were friends at college and got married almost immediately after Graduation. Their relationship is of friends rather than a husband and wife. They are the real couple goals for me. And that's exactly how I wish to marry. Thinking about this, I entered my room and looked at the clock. It said 9:15 pm, meaning I had 15 minutes to have Subhash back online. So, I went and took a nice shower. By the time I came out, mom arranged dinner for us on the table and they were waiting for me. After dinner, I helped her clean up the table and came back to my room.

I opened Orkut and looked at his chat. It said 'typing...' I bit my bottom lip, smiling, eagerly waiting for his message.

S: Hey...! You there?

V: Yup. Tell me.

S: You were telling me about your course and your college. Tell me more.

V: What else to say? I love what I'm doing so the work becomes easier. What about you? What did Subhash grow up into?

S: Whoa Lady! That's a deep question. It's a little too heavy for a first chat.'

V: Well. I would love to dive right in. I already missed a lot of your life. Also...Talking to you doesn't seem like a first-time thing... I know you!'

There was a huge chunk of silence after that message. I don't know what he was thinking. The word 'typing...' came and went many times, making me wonder what he was hesitating about. I wondered if I over spoke for a second. But no! I have always been like this with him. We never held back. We would talk about everything. There was a lot of comfort around him and the second I saw his message this afternoon, I felt all of that once again.

Suddenly, for the first time in many years, I remembered how lonely I felt when he left. I never shared with anyone but just packed that missing feeling and pushed it to the bottom-most part of my heart. And now that he is back, I never want to feel like that again. The urge to talk about everything that had happened every second for the last 10 years crawled through me. His message finally showed up.

S: I'm not sure. But my last memory of you was that you were crying when I told you we were leaving town and you wouldn't even look at me because you were so hurt. Honestly speaking I didn't understand your emotion back then. But believe me, I lived with that feeling, haunting me for every minute of every day for the last ten years.

V: Hmmm... I knew you didn't care. I thought I didn't mean enough for you to care. You were excited to move to Bangalore that leaving me and our friendship meant nothing to you.

S: As I said, I didn't think much of it. I thought you were overreacting. I was clouded with new excitement because my dad had been telling me about Bangalore like it was paradise. And I was only thinking about what it could mean to me. But I realized I missed you within the first few days. I missed us.

V: I think I get it. Oh, and hey! I was not overreacting. We were tight. I knew the value of such a friendship. I knew it was rare. And I missed you too.

S: Absolutely. I know that now.

Again, there was silence for five minutes. I wanted to lighten the mood so I just diverted the topic.

V: Hey... Did you join that cricket academy you mentioned? You were desperately waiting for that. You thought it could be great learning for your game.

S: Yes, I did. I still go there sometimes when I'm visiting. I'm surprised you still remember that...!

V: Haha I remember... There's a lot that has happened in the last few years. Relevant or not relevant, I want to tell you everything. Every minute detail.

S: I feel the same way too. Do you have a phone?

V: No. We can chat for now. I'll probably get a phone this year.

S: That's good to hear... Varna, we have a small party now. We are celebrating a friend's birthday on the hostel terrace. It's going to be an adventure, considering how strict our warden is. I will have to go now...

V: Okay... I would love to hear all about your adventure tomorrow then. Good night. And listen, I'm not letting you go this time.

S: Talk to you tomorrow. Not planning on leaving you. Ever again.

That comment brought a huge smile to my heart. It was almost 11:45 pm. With all that has happened today, I was in no mood to work. So, I retired for the night and went to sleep.

Chapter-2

My mom was preparing breakfast for us. My Dad was already sitting at the dining table, reading the newspaper, ready for breakfast. I got dressed up to go to college and packed my books for the day. And then the three of us had breakfast together. As I was heading out, my dad reminded me,

'Please wear your helmet madam.'

I gave him a thumbs-up and left. I love how my dad addresses me as 'Madam'. He not only calls me that but also believes it. He and my mom would come to me for any important decision that needs to be taken. They believe and value my thought process, due to which I have always felt validated, and it has also helped me think responsibly before I do something important in life.

As I was parking my bike in the parking lot of our university, I saw Akanksha entering the college. I waved at her, and she started walking towards me, waving back.

'Hey...! What's up?'

'I have to tell you something.'

I locked my helmet to my bike, and we both started walking towards the building.

'Guess who texted me on Orkut yesterday? I said excitedly, facing her and jumping in front of her with a huge smile on my face.

'Whoa! Aditya? Congratulations Dude!'

'Lower your voice, idiot. And no, it wasn't him.' I said, turning back and walking beside her again. I have had a huge crush on Aditya in my class since the very first day. I guess he and his friends know that for a fact. Because they keep yelling my name out whenever he enters the classroom.

'Then who else on this earth can get you that excited for?'

'You remember Subhash? My childhood friend. Their family left for Bangalore when I was in 4th grade...?'

'Subhash...? Doesn't ring a bell. Did you mention him before?'

'Of course, I did. How could I not? I told you he stayed in our community. My mom's colleague's son. We used to play together all the time.'

'Oh yeah... I remember now. So, he texted you huh?'

'Well, he saw my profile on Orkut and pinged me last night. It was so lovely catching up with him. I missed him so much you know. He was my best friend. And we almost picked up where we left off. I felt all of that closeness again.'

'Okay... Cool... But do I have to worry about this guy taking my place?'

'Hahaha...' I put my hand around her elbow holding her closer as we walked, 'Nah. You're always my best friend. But you need to know about him. He is important.'

'Important as in? Old best friend kind of important or potential boyfriend kind of important?'

That comment made me blush. I didn't realize there was this angle that I could think of. He was someone I knew well. I remember he was a cute kid, stylish. And he was from a good family. Thinking about having him for a boyfriend wouldn't be such a bad thing after all.

'Oh, my God... You are blushing!? How long do you know him for again? 12 hours? Wow!'

'No. It's nothing like that. I don't know what this could become. But I don't want to ruin it by adding pressure. For now, I'm extremely glad he is back in my life. There's a kind of comfort I had around him. And I would love to have that back. I want to have him as my best friend before anything else.' I said, as we both took our seats in the classroom and settled down. The Professor entered and just as the class was about to begin, Akanksha bent towards me and whispered,

'Whatever it becomes, please do know that I'm here with you, constantly. I'm not running away to Bangalore or anything. I'm the one who is here.'

I smiled looking at her and mouthing *Of course*.

Akanksha and I have struck up a great friendship since our first meeting. The very first time I saw her, she was alone in the canteen, with her bag and books filled on the table, and she was reading one of my favorite books. I instantly felt a strong connection with her and sat beside her at the same table. At first, she seemed a little pissed that I sat at her table without her consent, but later, when I started talking about that book, she was genuinely interested in the conversation. We shared similar interests, likes, and dislikes. Overall, we had a very unique vibe. We always felt nurtured in each other's presence. We always have deep and long conversations about so many general topics in life. It was the kind of friendship that made you grow as a person. For me, she was a perfect example of what a friend needs to be. She is a treasure I'm going to carefully preserve for as long as I'm alive. I believe that on some level, if not on this level, she feels the same way about me too.

So, when I'm seeing her jealous of Subhash, it's adorable. It's not like he is ever going to replace Akanksha in my life. Because even before I met her, I always had a huge place in my heart for Subhash. They have their separate compartments in my heart. And as I thought of all of this, I realized his, is as big as hers.

After a jam-packed day of classes, Akanksha suggested we finish our assignments at her place today. So, we both headed to her place.

As soon as we reached her house, Aunty welcomed us with a warm greeting. We both went into her room and closed the door. Her parents always allow and value privacy just as much as we'd appreciate it. My mom on the other hand is very curious. She believes too much privacy might spoil the child and it'd also make them feel like the child is withdrawing. So, at my house closing the door is never an option. As she entered the room, she put her bag on the floor, pulled another chair towards the system and asked me to sit. She opened Orkut.com and asked me to put in my credentials. I asked a little surprised,

'I thought we were supposed to finish our assignments?'

'Yeah, we'll get to that. Let me figure out Subhash first.'

When I opened my account, there was a message notification from Subhash which was sent just 10 minutes earlier.

S: Hey... I'm back from college early today. What time do you usually get back home? At what times do you have access to your system? Ping me asap.

I was controlling an overflowing smile and Akanksha caught it. She was nudging me playfully to reply to him. I couldn't wait to talk to him either.

V: Hey there! I'm back home by 4 pm.

S: Okay Nice... I'll be available online by 4 pm then. So, tell me, how was college today?

V: The usual. I told my best friend about you.

S: Wow. Varna talking about me to people huh? Why do I want to listen to that conversation!? How did it go? What did you say?

Right then Akanksha naughtily pushed me aside and started typing. I was yelling at her and pushing her away. But she was strong and fast enough to get up from her chair and sit on my lap covering my view of the system. I heard a 'sent' sound and I pushed her into her seat and looked at the system.

V: I told her you are my boyfriend.

Disaster! I banged my forehead with my fist and hit her on the shoulder. I saw *typing...* on the screen and started to worry. Before he could say anything, I replied quickly.

V: Hey. I'm sorry. That wasn't me.

It was Akanksha. My best friend from college. We came back to her place to finish a group assignment.

S: Oh...That's Okay. So, you didn't tell her I'm your boyfriend?

V: No...! Of course not. Why would I do that!?

S: You make it sound like it's such a bad thing. Would it be that bad?

I went blank for a second. Is he flirting with me now? Does he want me to be his girlfriend? We don't know much about our lives now. A lot has changed since he left. I grew up. There was a huge chunk of time that passed without his presence in my life. Same with him. I don't know what he grew up into. I can't go along thinking about a future with references I have from so far in the past. My smile and blush suddenly changed into worry and regret. Why would this stupid girl say something like that? I don't know how to remedy this without sounding rude.

I gasped when I heard Akanksha talking. I didn't realize she was standing right behind me watching the conversation. She said,

'What are you thinking?' He just asked if he can call himself your boyfriend. Say something...! Or maybe I should?'

She started typing something but I took over and started typing.

V: Hmm. I don't think it would be a bad thing. But it would be an unsure thing.

S: Meaning?

V: I missed you a lot, Subhash. I missed what would have been a wonderful friendship. Maybe if you didn't leave back then or maybe if we still kept contact, I could think about being boyfriend/girlfriend at this point. But you did leave. There's literally half of your life that I was not a part of. I would love to know you better first. Maybe we can have this conversation a few months later?

S: Hmmm... I would expect nothing less from you Varna. You have always been the more responsible, mature and grounded between the two of us. Anyway, I said it casually. Let's focus on being friends for now.

V: Yes. That'd be perfect. Hey... I'll finish homework, reach home and then text you, okay?

S: Sure. Bye.

I dropped my head on the table dramatically. Akanksha, who was waiting patiently on the bed, came running towards me and read the whole conversation.

'Well, we got one thing cleared. Isn't that easier for your further conversations?'

I looked up at her with narrowed eyes and an angry sigh.

'For what it's worth, he seemed like an interesting fella. Now look, there's no confusion as to what you would call each other anymore.'

'What are you talking about? It became more confusing than before. Because of that comment, you made it clear that that's where we are headed. What if this doesn't work out?'

'Oh, Come on! Let's worry about that later. For now, let's stalk his profile!'

There are very few pictures of him on Orkut. Most of them were food pictures, a few with a group of friends and there is one picture which is a close-up of him looking directly at the camera. There...He...Was. Oh Man... Is he Beautiful? or Is he Beautiful...!? My mind completely lost control over my face. My lips started to spread themselves over my cheeks, my cheeks jumping up due to the lips' force. My temple started to expand and my eyebrows raised and started dancing on my forehead. I shook my head, not believing what I just saw. I covered my cheeks with my palms to control this chaos and stop the movement my head started to make.

Akanksha stopped scrolling when she saw this picture. She leaned back onto the chair and looked at the screen admiring it. She didn't notice the tsunami that just occurred within me. Appreciatively nodding her head, she said, 'Hmm... I think I have a crush on your boyfriend...!' I laughed.

'He's not my boyfriend.... yet'. Well, that came out without my permission. I realized what I said and regretted it immediately.

'That's my girl...! You put that option open, okay?'

'Fine. Now shall we finish our assignment?'

I had to divert the topic and my mind. I never thought a picture, just a picture, could overwhelm me so much. But I can't let this deviate me from my goal. We started working and we finished our work before the time we thought we could. Akanksha was quite surprised by the kind of commitment and interest with which I finished my part. We are competitive like that. We would set a time to finish tasks and we would race. We did great during our combined study sessions. She was equally passionate about Arts, just like me. So, we usually feed off each other's passion. But today she saw something different in me. My mind was working twice as fast and creatively as it usually does. It felt like he gave me a high. I loved that feeling. I love that he had a positive effect on me.

I packed my bag, high-fived and proceeded to the living room. She came to the elevator to send me off. There was an aunty in the elevator from the floor above. Akanksha greeted her. I waved at Akanksha and just as the elevator took me to the floor below, she yelled at me,

'Say Hi to your boyfriend, from me!'

I tightened my fists and looked up at her angrily. By the time I was about to say something she disappeared. I slowly lowered my head. I could feel the angry gaze of the aunty from behind. As soon as we reached the ground floor, I pulled the first grill door and the second as fast as I could and ran towards my bike.

By the time I reached home, Mom was preparing dinner and I was welcomed with the delicious smell of my favourite food, sambar rice. I hugged her from behind and said,

'Can't wait to eat that Maa...! I have been smelling this from the ground floor.'

'Don't be ridiculous. There's no way you can smell it from three floors below. Go and freshen up. I will serve this in 15 mins. Nanna is on the way back from his office too. Let's have dinner together before you go off into your room and begin to "brainstorm."'

She said that with air quotes because I keep asking her to not disturb me when I'm creating something. When she would ask what I'm doing, I would say 'brainstorming', which is like a code word for us that I'm not supposed to be disturbed.

It took me forever to shower and dress up. I'm never like this. Today feels different. I'm feeling a little above myself. His face kept showing up like a flash every few seconds. I'm typically not very easy to impress. But he has the most beautiful smile on the entire planet. His eyes had so much purity in them. There was a kind of honesty in his appearance. I remember he was cute but was he this handsome? How did I miss that? That smile... Why is it so special?

I finished dinner and sat in front of my system, wanting to text him. It was almost 9 pm. He was online. I hesitated a little bit but I started the conversation,

V: Hey! I'm back. How are you doing?

How are you!? What's wrong with you Varna? You spoke to him just 4 hours ago. What would have changed? I hit my head with my fist.

S: I'm great. Haha... So, finished your work?

V: Yes. We did. Akanksha asked me to say Hi to you.

S: Oh, she did? She seems nice... Hi her back. Or maybe give me her Orkut ID. I'll say Hi.

V: Nope. That's not necessary. So... Did you have dinner?

Was I feeling possessive? That's not like me.

S: Yes, I had Pav Bhaji.

V: Pav Bhaji for dinner? That's odd. I like it but as an evening snack.

S: A friend got it for me. Anyway, do you remember how messy I was around food? I used to give hell to my mum. That's one thing that has changed in the last few years. I became a big Foodie. Food is Love.

V: Wow. That's good. Do you cook too?

S: Not really. I'm more interested in the process that goes behind getting the best food onto your plate.

V: Nice. Food is your passion then?

S: I guess.... I have never thought about it that way. I don't know. It could just be the love of hanging out with my friends. I'm not sure.

We continued the conversation for over two hours. We drifted from passion to interests to hobbies, friends and a lot more. He loves food. He loves to play Table tennis and Cricket. He loves movies just as much as I do. His life revolves around his friends. He told me about a few of his friends. We talked about me visiting Vizag sometime with my friends. He offered to be our guide and show us the best food joints in the town. I asked him when he would visit Hyderabad. He said three months later. I couldn't wait to meet him.

It was almost 15 minutes past 11. My dad gently knocked on my door, leaning on the frame and looking at me.

'Hello, Madam. It's 11 pm. I'm retiring for the night. When are you going to sleep?'

'10 minutes Nanna. I'm just shutting down.'

That night I went to bed, smiling, thinking about him. He had a knack to grasp your attention and make good conversation. Every second with him seemed interesting. His eyes kept flashing in front of me again. That picture ruined me. I slept onto the side and was looking at the wall. There he was, sleeping right beside me, looking directly into my eyes, smiling with those beautiful lips. I gasped and then shook my head. He vanished. I rolled my eyes and rolled onto my back. There he was, on the ceiling, looking at me and smiling. I closed my eyes and let out a long breath. There he was again, inside my eyes not letting me sleep. I tightened my eyes and put a pillow on my face, trying not to allow him inside. But he was already so deep inside, that every inch of my body felt his presence.

Chapter-3

The next morning when I woke up, his face flashed again. I smiled and stretched on my bed, turning and looking at the clock. I'm half an hour late. The smile vanished and I woke up with a jerk and ran into the shower. I grabbed an apple and proceeded to college.

As I was reaching my seat, Akanksha said dramatically using hand gestures,

'There it is...! That glow of new Love.'

'What are you talking about?'

'You know... Puffy eyes, dark circles... Couldn't sleep last night huh?'

I rubbed my eyes with my fingers and fake cried into my palm, 'Urgh... Is it that obvious? I couldn't get him out of my head. We chatted for 2 hours last night and I went to sleep. But he came along too! He is disturbing me more than I thought.'

We finished classes and I came back home as fast as I could and sat in front of the system, hoping to talk to him again. He wasn't online. I pinged him on Orkut and I waited for half an hour. No response. It was almost 5 pm and I was feeling impatient and restless. I was rotating in my chair, tapping on the table, shaking my legs. I placed my elbow on the table and rested my face on my palm. I kept looking at his chat. I started reading the entire conversation we had since we started talking. It was 6:15 pm and still no response. Anger took over. He promised he'd be online by 4 pm every day. *Did he forget? Don't I mean enough for him to at least let me know if he is busy with something?* I started to wonder; does he have a cell phone? He asked me if I had a phone but he didn't tell me if he did. I got up from my seat and started walking across the room to divert myself. As nothing was working out, I left the room.

I went into the kitchen and stood beside my mom, leaning on the kitchen platform. I was looking at the boiling milk, staring towards it but not looking directly at it. My vision was a blur. My thoughts were somewhere else. My mom was busy moving from the stove to the fridge to the sink, cleaning vegetables to make us dinner. While she was near the fridge, the milk boiled and fell over the vessel and turned off the flame. I was still looking at it but staring into nothingness. Just then my mom smelled the gas and milk and came running into the kitchen. She saw me staring at it and slapped me on my head. I shook my head and came back into consciousness and I yelled at her, 'What...!?'

'What? Are you kidding me? Where's your head at woman? Why didn't you off the stove?'

She yelled back pointing at the mess that the milk made falling all over the stove and onto the platform. I looked at it and realized what just happened. Regret took over my face. 'I'm sorry Maa. I was thinking about some assignment from today's class.' I lied. 'Please let me clean this up. You go and cut the vegetables. I will get this ready like fresh and new in 10 minutes. Is that okay?' I smiled at her with all my teeth. She looked at me with furrowed eyes, but nodded and went into the dining room. I let out a sigh and searched for a cloth to clean.

My mind was messed up. *What's wrong with me? Why am I becoming this desperate?* Just as I finished cleaning the platform, I heard a ping on my system. My face lit up like a 100-watt bulb. My mom looked at me doubtfully as I was running into my room. I sat in my chair and looked at the system but my smile faded away. It wasn't him. I threw my head onto the headrest of my chair and thought to myself,

Varna... This doesn't look healthy. Yesterday you believed he had a positive effect on you and your work. But today you are so disturbed that you are not able to concentrate at all. Not just on your work but on life, your regular real life. Step down from the clouds. You can't achieve your goals with this. Your ambition needs a hell of a lot more. It deserves every single bit of you. Someone from so long ago cannot take you away from your goal. Take it slow Varna.

I sat straight and closed Orkut. I opened my assignment and started working on it, feeling fresh. I asked my mom for a strong coffee and started sketching some ideas. After almost three hours I looked at all the work I got done and felt proud of myself.

This is it. This is the real high in life. Designing, creating something new out of thin air. Learning how to pour life into my designs and watching them take shape. This is what I want in life, more than anything.

With that thought, I went to bed.

The next day as I entered college, I saw Akanksha smiling and waiting for me in my parking spot. I parked my bike and we both started walking towards the classroom. She curiously asked me,

'What happened yesterday? Did you talk to him again?'

'Nothing happened. We didn't chat yesterday.'

'What? Why?'

'What do you mean why? It's not a job. That I need to check in every day and give and take updates.'

'Okay... Did something happen?'

'Well, he wasn't online. And I wasted way too much time on him that I realized I was going overboard with this relationship.'

'Okay... Tell me more.'

'I didn't like that feeling of losing myself. So, I decided to take things slow and not get too excited about him. I'm not even thinking about him.'

'And that makes you happy? Not thinking about him?'

'Yes. Absolutely. I don't care about him. My goal is of utmost importance.'

I lied to myself and her. I realized that I was lying because the moment I said that his face flashed in front of me and I felt weak in my knees. My heart skipped a beat. It physically hurt to say that I don't care about him. Because I do. He filled himself in my heart, body and soul without my consent. But I can't let this affect my goal. So, I'm going to pretend to be okay. At least till I finish my exams next month. Akanksha looked at me. She saw me thinking and she smiled, 'If you say so.'

She knew what I was thinking. We are close like that. She can read my thoughts. And she is the kind of friend everyone needs. I know she will support me in whatever path I choose to take.

That evening I went to Akanksha's place to finish my studies, because if I went home, I might change my mind. She knew I needed this. She didn't even attempt to turn on the computer. We fixed tasks and finished studying within the time we set for each other. After we finished our homework, we decided to watch a movie. I called my home landline and informed Maa that I would be late. Akanksha's mom, made *Aloo Bajjis* for us to munch on while we enjoyed the movie.

By the time I reached home, it was almost 10 pm. My mom served dinner for me and sat beside me talking about how her day went and asking me about mine. I told her about the movie I watched with Akanksha. After dinner, I helped her clean up and she proceeded to bed. I stopped in front of my room and looked at my computer. I was tempted to run inside and tell him everything. About my day and how inspired I felt after my class today and about the movie, I saw with Akanksha. I wanted to tell him how close I still am to my parents. I wanted to tell him what I'm looking for in a relationship, what I like and what I don't. I wanted us to have a relationship. I felt strongly drawn to him. I went inside and switched on the system. As I excepted and hoped, he did text me.

S: Varna... Hi.

S: I saw your messages. I'm here now.

S: You there...?

S: I'm sorry. I should have informed you. I was helping out a friend with something.

And he was still online. My heart started dancing. I replied,

V: Hey... I'm here.

S: Varna...! Thank God. I thought you were angry with me. I'm sorry.

My ears suddenly craved to listen to him call my name.

V: Why would I be angry? It's not like we are in a relationship. Relax!

I lied. Of course, I was angry. But I thought to myself it's too early to show my true colours.

V: Helping out a friend huh? What is it?

S: She is a senior. She needed help with finishing up some pending work. So, I assisted her.

V: Senior girl! huh? She must be elder than you.

S: Haha of course. We are good friends though.

V: Cool...

It was almost clear that it was bothering me.

S: So... How was your day?

V: Great. Akanksha and I watched Pilla Zamindar.

S: Hey. I watched it with my friends recently. Great movie. Do you like Nani?

V: I loveeeee him. He is my favourite actor.

S: Mine too! I love Surya also.

V: Aw I love Surya too. My other favourite actor! But Nani is my forever!

S: I remember how much your family loved movies. We used to go together remember?

V: Of course.

S: Maybe we should plan something like that when I visit. Yeto Vellipoyindi Manasu will release when I'm there probably. Let's watch that together. You love Nani. I love Sam!

V: Sure. It would be great.

I remembered that I wanted to take things slow. So, I decided to retire for the night as it was already late.

V: Hey. I need to go sleep now. I have an early class tomorrow.

S: Yup. Go ahead. I'll see you in your dream.

V: Hahaha. Funny! Good night, Subhash.

Chapter-4

I just came home from my morning jog and started making filter coffee. I served it in two mugs with our names on them, a gift from our sons for our anniversary. I took the coffee mugs into the balcony where he was just finishing his yoga routine. The balcony was almost like a room, 10'X10' with a beautiful view overlooking the beach. As I walked in, he came and sat on the wicker chair on one side of the balcony and I took the other. He took his mug and read the headlines of the newspaper, giving me general news updates. Just then our grandchild came running into the balcony wishing us Good Morning and sat on my lap. I kissed and hugged him while his mom came in with a tray carrying his milk and tea for her and her husband, my son. We all sat together and were drinking our beverages when my other son came home from his morning run. They were identical twins. He brought his protein shake into the balcony and sat with us. My grandson immediately dropped down from my lap and went and sat with my second son. After a little while we all dispersed and became busy with our schedules. My husband and my second son, who was going to take over our business, were discussing different ideas for business growth. I got freshened up and started for my work in my car and on the way, I dropped my grandson near the bus stop where his school bus would come and pick him up. I looked back at the bungalow. It was a beautiful two-storeyed individual house with lots of open spaces and a spacious garden. There he was, Subhash, looking at me from the balcony. When I smiled and waved at him, he threw a flying kiss and waved back.

I woke up from my sleep with a gasp and slowly sat up realizing it was a dream. My mom who was boiling milk in the kitchen, came into the bedroom, seeing me awake,

'Good morning, Varna. Do you have any homework you need to finish? You woke up at 5:30am.'

I looked at her with half-opened eyes, feeling drowsy.

'No Maa. A dream woke me up.'

'Oh... A nightmare?'

A smile took over my face, replaying the dream I just had.

'It was a delightful dream. I'll go back to sleep. Please wake me up in an hour.'

'Okay. The dreams that come in the early morning hours usually come true...!'

I was startled by that comment. The smile on my face refused to leave as I lay on the bed with my hands behind my head and stared at the ceiling. I took in that moment and closed my eyes. It's been two months since I reconnected with Subhash. I have been completely obsessed with him ever since.

I came to college a little early. When Akanksha entered the classroom, she was shocked that I was already there. She saw me smiling to myself and said,

'Hello! You came early! What are you dreaming about?'

'Subhash...'

'Ohh, Okay...'

I turned towards her and said, 'My heart isn't in my control anymore. He was in my dream last night.'

'Wow! Did anything good happen? Did you kiss? Tell me everything. I want details.'

'I wish it was just a romantic dream. I would have thought, I'm very much attracted to him and left it alone. But it wasn't.'

'Then what was it?'

'I saw a future... Akanksha.' I let out a happy laugh that I have been holding in. 'I saw this beautiful life we created. A family... A house overlooking the sea! We had twin boys! One of them was married and we had a grandson too...! It was really amazing.'

'Oh god...! You do realize that it's just a dream, right? Don't get over-excited. You guys are not even in a relationship...!'

'I know. But I realized that's exactly where I want to be. I realized... I'm in Love with him.'

As soon as I said it out loud, it felt so real and validated. I love him. I do. I want him in my life. I want to keep exploring him and have him as my partner.

'That's great... But remember what you told yourself about taking it slow. It might end up differently than you are imagining. Let things unfold on their own. I just don't want to see you get hurt; you know.'

'Yeah of course. I understand. Thankyou.'

'I don't mean to divert you or anything but Aditya has been staring at you for a while now. Don't look!'

Of course, I turned immediately and was kind of surprised to see that was true. He was looking in this direction but he turned away the second I saw him. Akanksha threw her head on the table feeling embarrassed.

'Whoa...! What is this turn of events? All these years I have followed him around letting him know that I was interested in him. Just as I have taken myself out of the market, he develops an interest in me. That's something!'

We both laughed. Me and Akanksha proceeded to the canteen after college hours to get a cup of coffee. We sat at our favourite table, the table where we first met. We were giggling about a joke Akanksha just made when Aditya entered the canteen. He usually never comes to the canteen. He entered searching for someone and stopped scanning the room the minute he saw us. We realized that now we were looking directly at him and him at us. We stared for a few seconds and I turned back, packed my bag and stood up to leave the canteen signalling Akanksha to follow me. She did so and he kept staring at us as we walked past him, maybe not knowing how to start a conversation.

We came out and walked towards my bike, laughing and enjoying this new attention I was getting. Akanksha looked back at the canteen when she was about to get on the bike and saw that he was still staring at us.

Aditya is a fairly attractive guy. 6' tall, dusky skin tone, perfectly crafted shoulders and arms. One could easily tell he works out. For all that machismo, he was not very good with girls. He intentionally kept himself away from all the attention. He would always distance himself from the girls in our class too! But today was different. We didn't understand it but knowing him, it could have been something as simple as him wanting to borrow some notes.

That night I mentioned Aditya to Subhash. We were having a conversation about crushes, previous relationships, what type of men/women are we generally attracted to and that kind of stuff. He mentioned he had a crush on his super senior when he joined college but she passed out this year. He mentioned almost all my characteristics to be 'his type'. And I intentionally mentioned everything exactly opposite to how he looked as 'my type'. He didn't know we saw his picture. He seemed genuinely upset and jealous for a little while. I was enjoying seeing him like this.

S: Okay. So, you are saying you like dusky men with a muscular look. But what if you found someone close to your heart but doesn't fit into that image?

V: I just wouldn't be physically attracted to him.

I was laughing and enjoying this way too much.

S: Anyway, tell me... If you could have only one food item for the rest of your life, what would that be?

He diverted the topic completely. I empathised with him so I went along.

V: Hmmm can I say chocolates? I love chocolate. What about you?

S: Haha. Rice and pappu maybe... Mom's an amazing cook and strangely she had gotten even better after I moved out of the house. So unfair. I miss her cooking.

V: Aww. That's sweet.

S: Hey do you have a landline at your house?

V: Yes. Of course.

S: I want to hear your voice Varna.

My heart started beating faster than I have ever known. The heat generated in my body made all the water evaporate and I was feeling thirsty. I gulped and ran to the fridge to grab a bottle of water. I put my face into the freezer and breathed with my mouth to calm myself. After I have settled down, I looked at the clock. It was 11 pm and both my parents were asleep. I walked slowly towards my room, thinking and strategizing. He was probably wondering what this silence meant. He didn't text me back. I typed my landline number.

V: Give me 30 seconds. I'll close my parents' bedroom door. I'll lift the call on the first ring. I don't want to disturb them.

I was sitting beside the phone, rubbing my palms. When the phone rang, I lifted it immediately but couldn't say a word.

'Hello…'

'Varna? Are you there?'

It was so overwhelming. Until that moment, I have fallen in love and imagined a future with someone through the computer. I typed things and it replied and I had time to blush, type, retype and carefully blend what I wanted to say. Now, listening to his voice for the first time, made everything feel so damn real. It felt like giving life to the imaginary thing I have created in my head. I wasn't sure anymore if I can hide my feelings over a phone call. And his voice… I didn't know I could fall in love with someone's voice. I never thought I could fall in love with my own name hearing it from someone's voice. My name sounded beautiful when he called me. Thinking about all this, my voice just refused to show up. It probably felt weak and intimidated. His was the most beautiful voice my ears have ever had the privilege of hearing. I just couldn't fathom the extent of how much he affected me and my body. I couldn't even say hi. I put the phone down and pressed it against the box in a stupid hope of containing the river of emotions I was feeling.

The phone rang again. It kept ringing. I didn't bother that it would wake my parents up. I took a breath to gather myself and lifted the call,

'Hello,' My voice felt weaker than ever. I cleared my throat.

'Varna? Was that you before?'

'Yeah. It was me. Sorry, I cut the call.'

'Never mind. Is this okay with you? A phone call... I mean.'

'Yeah, why?'

'It's just I'm not very fond of typing so much continuously. Also, I could talk a lot more if we are on call. And I wouldn't need to use the common laptop for all our roommates. They are kind of complaining about how much I use it.'

'Hahaha. This is okay. I'm not sure I can talk to you if my parents are awake, though. They would ask too many questions.'

'Oh, God. I didn't know someone's laughter could bring me so much joy. You have the best and most amazing laughter sound I have ever heard.'

I instantly blushed and pressed the phone against my cheek, wanting to bring his voice closer than it already was. I pretended to ignore the compliment and continued the conversation.

'But we can talk for a little while after they sleep and before I sleep. If that's okay with you.'

'Of course! I would wait the entire night if it means I get to talk to you.'

I was liking this side of him. On text, he was not this flirtatious. He was playing this field so damn well and I'm falling in love with every word that came out of him. *Should I tell him I love his voice? Maybe not...*

'I wouldn't do that to you. Having a good night's sleep should be a priority.'

'You and your concern, Varna. You always used to amaze me how you took care of all of us in the gang back then too.'

'Did I take care of you? Why do I not remember that?'

'Probably because that comes so naturally to you.'

'Hahaha.'

'I could tell you all the jokes I know. Damn, I would strive to become a comic to hear you laugh like that.'

I laughed again. I loved to see how much I'm affecting him too. Because that's only fair, he filled every cell in my body with just his voice. I began to wonder what would become of me if I met him directly. I would probably faint.

'Varna... I recently started working with my friend, Gowtham. He has this fusion food joint here in Gajuwaka. I'll be there most of my evenings.'

'Oh okay... That's something you are interested in, right? Food business?'

'Yes... I thought it would be great to have field experience.'

'Of course.'

We talked for about half an hour. He made me smile, laugh and blush many times. When I said I had to sleep, there was a few seconds of silence which we both felt was filled with so much love we had for each other. We ended the conversation planning our phone calls, what time they should start and how many rings, secret codes and details like that.

The next morning, I entered the class, excited to tell Akanksha about our phone call. I frowned with surprise when I noticed Aditya looking at her. The moment he saw me, he turned away. A few months earlier something like this would have meant a lot to me. But now I couldn't care less. I settled in my seat and started talking.

'You know what happened last night?'

'Oooh... Tell me.'

'We spoke. Over the phone...!!!'

'Whoa. That's new. Tell me more.'

'Dude... his voice! It penetrated my heart and stabbed it. Deep and bold yet gentle and sweet. Puberty did so much good to him.'

'Wow. What did you guys talk about? Did you confess your feelings to him?'

My smile kind of faded away. I took a deep breath and said,

'No. I don't think I can. I don't want to mess this up. I don't have the power or energy to lose him again. I love where we are. I love our conversations. Light and fun. Nothing much to worry about! Also, commitment and real relationship is all serious stuff, isn't it? We need to think about a lot of different things to decide to spend the rest of our lives together. It is too much. I like just being in love. I'm enjoying every bit of this phase.'

Akanksha lifted her eyebrows and turned her face nodding to herself.

'Okay... If you say so. Did you ever feel this way about Aditya?'

I was shocked to hear that question.

'What...!? No! Why would you ask that?'

'I don't know. You said you had a crush on him and I saw you feeling butterflies in your stomach when he's around. But I guess THIS is different. You seem surer about Subhash. But I just wanted some clarity.'

'Crush! Akanksha...' I let out an angry sigh, not believing what she just said, 'I still think Aditya is a very attractive man. But it's just a crush. With Subhash, it's not like that. I know him. We shared a beautiful friendship before. We would spend all our days and nights together in our summer holidays. He used to tease me. We would go to the movies together. We would argue about who was better. We also cared a lot about each other. He was very protective you know, him being two years elder than me. And to lose that friendship was devastating to me. I didn't know what that was back then but I have gone through a phase of depression after he left. It took me an entire year to be myself again and make new friends and accept the new reality.

And Oh, dear god, the way he has changed...! His looks...ugh! He became so tall and handsome. He is a man now. And that voice... I'm madly in love with him.'

As I was telling her all this, I realized how deeply I'm invested in him now and how hard I've been clinging to this past memory of him and imagining a future with him. Suddenly it all felt so scary and overwhelming. Akanksha didn't expect me to react that way when she asked that question, but it helped me figure out where I was regarding our relationship. All the memories that I dug deep into my heart, rushed back up and disturbed me.

'Okay... I'm sorry if I said something wrong. I didn't know how big a part he was, in your life before. I just thought he was an old friend. But I understand now why you are so shaken by his presence in your life again.'

I didn't even pay attention to what she was talking about. I never told anyone how much I missed him when he left. I became so silent and my parents were worried about me at that point. I didn't want to see them like that so I just pushed all the pain and hurt deep down and locked it in a safe box for all these years. Maybe now that he is back in my life, I felt the need to finally open it up and deal with it. I stood up, grabbed my bag and walked out of the classroom before the class started and Akanksha followed me.

We sat in our regular place in the canteen. Akanksha brought us two cups of coffee and samosas. I didn't bother to touch any of them as I was deep in thought. Then Akanksha lifted the plate of samosas and started making circles in the air around my nose. I looked at her in slow motion. She started acting all goofy to divert me. When I finally smiled, she sat back in her chair with a sigh of relief. We had the samosa and coffee and waited in the canteen for another hour hoping to get back to the class later.

As we were casually chitchatting, I noticed Aditya entering the canteen and walking towards us. 'Hey Akanksha, why weren't you in the class today? The professor gave us a new assignment and you are in our group.'

We were in shock that Aditya was talking to us! I was surprised that he completely ignored me and was talking to Akanksha. I decided to pull his leg for a little while.

'Why. Didn't you miss me in the class? Only her?'

'Ummm... No... I mean... It's just that we are in the same group and I wanted to discuss our course of action.'

He looks terrified of me. It's so funny. Akanksha hid her face behind my head, controlling her laughter.

'Just her?'

'Actually No. You, Akanksha, me and Srikar.'

'Oh Well. Isn't that a perfect group!?'

He couldn't look directly into my eyes. I felt pity for him, so I cut out the act.

'Hey. Relax. I was just kidding. We can discuss this over lunch. Is that okay?'

He felt better that even a small hint of a smile came onto his face. He nodded and left the canteen.

That evening I headed to Akanksha's place. We finished our homework and I rushed back home. By the time I came home and freshened up, he texted me on Orkut and was waiting for me. We talked about how the day went. I told him I have finally spoken to Aditya today. He asked me for details about how the conversation went. It was evident that he was jealous. I felt bad for him so I told him clearly that I was over my crush and we are just classmates now who happened to be working in the same group for a term project.

I finished dinner and was desperately waiting for my parents to go to sleep. A few minutes after they went inside their room, I slowly closed the door. I asked Subhash to call and waited on the phone.

I was imagining myself in a fantasy land, sitting on a white fluffy cloud and talking to him with a phone that looked like a crescent moon. I felt love in the air, every second of our conversation.

Chapter-5

As we finished the fourth semester and were just back to college after the holidays, we were enjoying our favourite canteen samosas, sipping coffee and chitchatting. Aditya, Akanksha and I became good friends in the last four months and we hung out together all the time. Srikar slowly moved out of the group having different priorities than us. But we stuck with each other. We became thicker than I have ever expected us to be. In the holidays, we went to the movies and an amusement park and they came by to my place to have lunch a couple of times. We usually gather at Akanksha's place as Adi stays very close by. Akanksha and Adi played badminton on the streets now and then. She invited me to their games many times and I would go but I would end up talking to Subhash for hours on her landline phone. Both of Akanksha's parents were working, so the house would be free for me to talk to him for as long as I wished. Subhash and I became a lot closer too. We talked almost every night and many times during the day too. He was supposed to come to Hyderabad in the holidays but instead, he visited his parents in Bangalore. I was upset that I didn't get to meet him but I understood he was missing his mom so didn't say or ask him anything.

I was lost in thought until Aditya snapped his finger in front of my face to get me back,

'So? When are you introducing us to your guy?'

'Soon, I hope. I don't think he has any plans to visit anytime soon though.'

'If I had a girlfriend in another city, I would visit her like once every month.'

I felt a pinch in my heart when he said that. But I didn't let it show. I frowned and nudged his arm with my elbow.

'Come on, Adi. First of all, I'm not his girlfriend...' Adi and Akanksha raised their eyebrows and folded their hands. I looked at them and rolled my eyes giving up.

'Okay. Let me rephrase that. I don't know if he thinks I'm his girlfriend. We never got to that, yet. And he has been busy. I told you he was working at his friend's food store.'

'Hmmm... Remind me again. Why aren't you guys boyfriend/girlfriend yet?'

I paused for a second. I don't know the answer to that either. We have been back together for over 6 months now. I have been madly in love with him for almost the same time. We do talk about how much we miss each other and how important we are to each other but he never confessed if he loves me and neither did I. To be honest we never felt the need to. We know how much love we have for each other and that it can fill the planet if we decide to spread it. At this point, Akanksha interfered in the conversation,

'Adi... Just leave her alone, will you? Let's go. It's time for class.'

I looked at Akanksha and smiled thanking her in my head. She winked and started walking out of the canteen. I put on my bag and just as I was about to move, Adi who was right behind me, held my bag, hence stopping me from walking any further. I almost fell back because I was not expecting that. I gasped and looked back at him almost yelling at him, 'What!?'

He pulled me back and ran ahead of me and said, 'I'm first.' I burst into an unexpected laughter and ran behind him.

Aditya is silly like that. He looks all macho but he is just a little kid at heart. He would tease me; he would pull my leg about Subhash. He would constantly make it a point to make me angry with something or the other and then he would give that goofy smile of his, which would melt my heart. I guess I deserve that for all the torture I have put him through in the first two years. He is very sweet at heart and sometimes he genuinely sounds happy for me and Subhash. Almost like a relief...!

After a full day of classes, Akanksha came running to me as I starting my bike and said,

'Hey. Leaving already? I thought we could hang out at my place. Adi was saying we could order pizza.'

'No... I want to get home. It's been 5 days since I talked to Subhash you know. He has been very busy. He was supposed to call me last night wishing me luck for the first day back to college. But he didn't. I'm hoping he left me a message. You guys go ahead. I wouldn't mind.'

'He doesn't call until 11 pm when Aunty and Uncle are at home, right? Why don't you join us? You can reach home by 6 pm.'

'Mom and Dad went to Warangal for a wedding. It'll be late by the time they come back. I told him they'd be gone. So, we planned a call today.'

'Okay then. I'll see you Monday.'

'Monday? What about tomorrow?'

'Of course, you forgot. I told you about my cousin's housewarming. That's tomorrow.' She turned and walked away.

'Okay... Bye.'

Something didn't feel right about that conversation. Maybe she was upset that I'm cancelling a lot on her. But I couldn't miss this opportunity to talk to him. I have already been missing him way too much.

I was sitting on the couch and waiting for his call munching on a snack. It was almost after an hour that he finally called,

'Hey, Varna. I'm so sorry. Did I keep you waiting?'

'Yes, you did. What happened? You are an hour late.'

'I had to pick something up for the store. I was out shopping all day.'

'Hmmm... I don't understand this at all. You are always working in the store. Aren't you missing classes? Aren't you missing your friends?'

'No. I'm working for my own good Varna. I gain more than he does with this arrangement.'

'Fine. So, you know what happened today? Adi and I tried to pull a prank on Akanksha...' he cut me off mid-sentence.

'Varna, please. I don't have time for this. Talk to me only if it's important.'

Silence... That hurt very bad and deep. I never heard him that rude before. I felt like a meteor just hit me. I could sense the frustration in his voice. For the last five months, he had been very busy and spoke to me only twice or thrice a week. Even the times we spoke, he would rush through the conversation. *Is he frustrated with me? Or work? Or the fact that he is not able to spend time? Did I become too clingy for him?*

'Am I wasting your time, Subhash?'

He hesitantly replied, 'No...'

When I didn't respond, after what felt like a solid minute, he said, 'Listen Varna, I'm so sorry.'

'No. You meant yes. I know you have been busy and all. But I thought you were genuinely waiting to talk to me too Subhash.'

'No. Of course, I was. I love talking to you Varna. It's just that I'm not in the right head space right now. I'm sorry I said that.'

'Fine. I have things to do too. I'll talk to you later. Bye.'

I cut the call before he said anything. I felt like I wrapped myself and handed it over to him and he just crushed me and threw me in the bin. I didn't realize how much my days and nights were filled with him. His calls, his texts, his voice, his thoughts. I'm completely obsessed with him. Maybe I came on too strong for him. I didn't like this feeling. I didn't like being put down. That's not a good thing in my culture. I need to pick myself up for my sanity. So, I went into my study room and started working.

The phone rang again. Three rings, which was our secret code, and stopped. I didn't call him back. I just closed my eyes and ears and let the tear, that was lingering in my eye, fall off my face. The phone rang in our secret code again and again. I didn't move an inch from my place. I exhaled through my mouth and switched on my computer. I was determined to give myself some space. I didn't bother the ringing phone and started working.

After about half an hour, I got curious about what he had to say. So, to check if he texted, I logged into Orkut.

S: Varna. I'm sorry.

S: You know how much you mean to me. I'm sorry I snapped at you. You don't deserve that sweetheart.

S: You are not a waste of time. You are my relief, my comfort. After a heavy working day, you are the only thing that can relax me. I would wait all day to come running back to you.

S: Please call me back...

I instantly cooled down and a smile escaped my lips. *Did he just call me sweetheart?* That's so sexy. I suddenly felt the need to hear him say *I love you.* It is obvious in our conversations that there is love and care. But we never said it aloud. *Should I tell him first?*

I decided against it.

V: Subhash. It's ok. I'm not angry anymore. But I have work too. I'll talk to you later.

I came offline and gathered myself together to get some work done. After an hour or so, Mom and Dad came back home. I sat with them listening to all the stories about the wedding and the relatives who asked about me and how my parents told them that it was my first day back to college so I couldn't make it. There was some disappointment from their end too, that I didn't attend the wedding, but they never said anything to me. They always gave me that space to choose and decide what to do for myself.

Chapter –6

I finished my work and waited by the phone, reading a book, trying not to feel the desperation of waiting for him. It has been a week since our first fight. I believe we have only become stronger.

When the phone rang, I threw the book aside and jumped to lift the call. We spoke about his work and how the food store was going on. I gave him updates about Akanksha, Aditya and our group assignments. He became quite comfortable with Adi in our conversations. At about 11:58 pm, he started to change the topic.

'Varna. I have to tell you something...'

I was squeezing the phone with the largest smile on my face. It was high time he came around and finally admitted his feelings towards me. I couldn't wait anymore to hear him say those three magical words.

'Tell me.'

'You are one of the most precious gifts the earth has ever had the privilege to bare. You are a blessing to everyone who can call you theirs. To me, you are the most special person in my life. Thank you for being born and being a part of my life. Happy Birthday, Varna...!'

He caught me off guard. I was completely surprised. Of course, I wished he would tell me *I love you* but this was special. We have been away from each other for 11 years now and he still remembers my birthday. My birthday started in the most special way possible with his beautiful wish. I was smiling so hard that I felt my lip ends poking into my cheeks.

'Oh my god... You remember?'

'Yes. I do. I have secretly wished you and thought about you on this day every single year for the last few birthdays that I wasn't with you. I remember...Varna.'

'I don't know what to say.'

'Then don't. Let's just leave it here. I have a surprise for you today.'

My face began to expand and so did my heart. *A surprise? What could it be? Is he coming to Hyderabad to meet me?* I couldn't imagine what would happen to me. I couldn't control my happiness.

'Oh, Subhash... What are doing to me...!?'

'Can you say my name again?'

I was feeling so overwhelmed. I could feel him, see him, sense him all around me even through a phone call. I closed my eyes and hugged the hand holding the phone with the other, feeling like I was hugging him. I really couldn't wait anymore. I wanted to tell him that I love him.

'Subhash...' I whispered.

There was silence. I don't know what he was thinking. *Is he anxious to meet me too? Is he anxious to tell me that he loves me?* I decided to tell him today that I love him more than he can ever imagine and I have decided that I'm going to spend the rest of my life with this man. For some reason, I was very convinced that I would be meeting him today.

'Subhash. I have a surprise for you too.'

'You do?'

'Yes. You will know by the end of the day.'

For an entire minute, we just kept listening to each other's breathing through the phone, feeling peaceful.

'Bye... Varna.'

'Okay... Bye. See you soon.'

I blurted out and cut the call. I bit my tongue for saying that. I hope he was not disappointed that I guessed his big surprise. I went to sleep with the happiest, warm and cosy feeling of love.

I woke up at around 6 am and was staring at the ceiling fan. It felt like the rotating fan was kind of hypnotizing me because my vision started to blur and I was imagining how this day was going to be. I'm going to meet Subhash today. Akanksha never fails to surprise me on my birthday and my parents told me they had a big gift for me too! Just as I was waking up from bed, my mom looked at me from the kitchen and yelled at my dad,

'Prakash…! She is up…! Come on.'

My mom and dad came into my room, Mom holding a plate with a diya, sindhoor and some oil. On every birthday my mom rotates this divine diya, the *harathi* around my head removing all the evil in my surrounding and puts the sindhoor on my forehead between my eyebrows, protecting me from all that is evil. Then she would take some oil and apply it on my head, which I should be cleaning off during my head bath with rose petals water. She would even give me some homemade de-tan mix to apply to my body. This whole ritual is being done to me on every single birthday for as long as I remember. They never failed to make me feel like a big diva on this day. I feel like a royal queen. My mom finished the ritual and then my dad followed too.

'Happy 21st birthday Bangaram. Go, freshen up and come on. We have a surprise for you…!' He said.

'Happy Birthday Kanna. May all your wishes for today and every single day for the entire year come true and may you be the happiest.'

I blushed and bent my head closing my eyes. Subhash's face flashed right in front of me. If everything I was wishing for today would have to come true, I will be meeting him today and I'm finally going to confess my feelings to him.

I brushed and bathed with a smile stuck on my face. I wore the new dress my mom bought for me. I looked in the mirror and blushed.

You are going to meet him today, you lucky girl. I said to myself in the mirror and came out into the dining room.

'You look beautiful Madam...!' My dad claimed.

My mom came forward, hugged me and kissed my forehead. She sat me down on the dining table chair and handed me a small box, perfectly wrapped and with a ribbon flower on top. I looked at her and frowned. I opened the wrapper and it was a cell phone! Samsung Champ, the latest version of the Samsung smartphone series. 2" screen, 2MP camera. My first own phone...!

I yelled at the top of my lungs and hugged my dad and mom together.

'Yayyy... A smartphone...!!!'

'Do you like it?' My dad asked.

'Like it? Are you kidding me? I love it...! Thank you so much, Nanna. Thanks, Maa. I love you guys so much.'

I hugged them again. I was the happiest. I love the fact that I have a phone of my own now but I'm happier that I can talk to Subhash whenever and wherever I want to. It would be great too, since I was going to confess my feelings today. We would have a lot more to talk and some things are just better talking and listening in the privacy of your bedroom rather than in the living room even though there is no one around you.

'Now finish your breakfast. We will visit the temple before you go to college.' My mom said. We all had breakfast together. My dad got me a sim card too. I by-hearted my phone number. I took some pictures of my mom and dad. I saved their phone numbers and Subhash's too. I wanted the first call from this phone to be to him. So, I went out into the balcony and dialled Subhash's phone number. When he picked up, I almost jumped with excitement.

'Guess who...!'

'Varna? Is that you?'

'Yess...!!!'

'Whose number is this?'

'Mine...! Amma Nanna got me a phone Subhash! This is my phone number. Save it.'

There was no response from the other side. Or maybe I didn't hear it because of all the excitement.

'Subhash? Ok Anyway. I can't talk now. I'll go to college and call you. Bye.'

I cut the call and looked at my phone oh, so proudly. I went back in, packed my bag and we all left the house together. We went to the temple in my colony and I left for college from there.

When I entered the classroom, to my surprise the entire classroom was empty. I looked back into the corridor. None of my classmates were there. The class was supposed to begin in 5 minutes. I started to wonder how can an entire class be late. As I was proceeding to the canteen to check, a junior came to me and asked if I was Varna. I said yes and she pointed towards the canteen. I thought that was weird and walked towards the canteen doubtfully. The windows were closed, which was not normal. The surroundings were awfully quiet. There were no lights too. When I entered the canteen...

'Surprise...!!!'

I was taken aback. The entire classroom was there. In the front were Akanksha and Aditya with party blowers in their mouths making noises. Some of them had birthday caps on their heads. Two other classmates of mine were holding a large banner that said 'Happy Birthday'. I laughed and hugged Akanksha. I was hundred per cent sure this was her idea. I don't know how she pulled off asking the entire classroom to be a part of this. There was a cake in one of the corner tables. It was the table where Akanksha and I first met. When I walked among them in between cheers and wishes, I felt like a celebrity. Adi came and put a special birthday hat on me. He hugged me from the side and wished me. I cut the cake and fed it to Akanksha first, then to Adi. I cut the remaining cake into small pieces and asked the canteen uncle to distribute it to all of them. When I asked Akanksha about the class, she said,

'We requested the professor to give us a half hour before we could return to class. So, we have about 10 minutes to hear your vote of thanks speech and finish the cake and rush into the class.'

I laughed and secretly thanked our professor too.

'Guys…Thank you so much for being a part of my celebration. I'm blessed to have the most amazing friends and the most supportive and wonderful classmates to have arranged this just to make me feel special. I know some of you might think this is a little too much, which it is! But you cannot imagine how much this means to me. So, thank you for coming along. I love you guys. And anything that you would like to have in the canteen today, it's on me. I'll tell the canteen uncle to open a tab in my name. Have a blast, guys.'

Everybody clapped and cheered for me. Akanksha looked at me with an appreciating smile and a small clap. I was a little surprised with myself for giving everyone a treat like that. But I was way too happy to contain myself. We left for the class and I thanked the professor for giving us that half hour.

After the end of the first session, we headed to the canteen again and ordered coffee and samosas. Just then a junior whom I know came in and called out for me. She saw me wave my hand at the corner and walked towards me,

'Varna… Someone is waiting for you at the gate.'

This is it. He came! Subhash is here. My face lit up like a 100w bulb. I jumped up almost spilling my coffee and ran towards the door. At the door, I slowed down and caught my breath. I looked at Akanksha, who gave me an assuring smile and a thumbs up. Her smile relaxed me a bit and I walked out. The gate was visible from the canteen. It was around 200m away but visible enough to know who you are looking at. The person waiting at the gate was standing turning the other way. I smiled and walked towards him. As I crossed half the distance to the gate, he turned towards me. My smile vanished. I looked at him confused. I even turned back to see if someone else was there that this person wants to meet because it wasn't Subhash. I stopped walking. He was looking directly at me. I wasn't sure if he knew who I was but he started walking towards me. As I was confident by now that that person didn't come to see me, I turned back and started walking back.

'Varna?' he called.

I looked back with a big question mark on my face.

'Yes?'

'Hi. This is Madhu. Subhash's friend.' He extended his hand in a handshake. I shook my hand and looked at him, surprised. *His friend? Why isn't he here?* This man was carrying a gift-wrapped box too, which was the size of a shoe box.

'I know you're expecting to see him. But he asked me to tell you he was not in a position to meet you. And he feels extremely bad about that.'

'Not in a position to see me meaning? What's wrong with him? Did something happen?'

'No. Nothing is wrong with him. Can we please sit and talk?'

He gestured towards the seating under a nearby tree. We went and sat there. I looked at the canteen and I saw Akanksha staring at me with a doubtful face. She knew it wasn't Subhash whom I met. She signalled me asking who I was with. I didn't respond. I turned my head towards him and asked him,

'If there is nothing wrong with him, why isn't he here himself? Is he here in Hyderabad?'

He started to feel nervous. He was looking behind me, almost staring. I suddenly looked back but no one was there.

'What is it, Madhu?'

'Ummm I'm sorry. Listen I really can't tell you anything. Please take this. This is a gift from Subhash. He asked me to deliver it to you. I don't know the answers to all your questions. He told me you'll know when you open it. Now I have to leave. Thank you. Bye.'

He placed the box in my lap, stood up and rushed to leave. I looked at him leaving and was about to say something but thought it was useless. I just looked at the box and wondered what was going on. Just then I heard him call my name so I turned,

'Happy Birthday.'

I smiled but he didn't. That wish was sad. Almost like apologizing for ruining my day. As I approached the canteen, Aditya started cheering for me. I didn't respond. Akanksha shushed him immediately. She understood something wasn't right. I handed the box to her, walked out of the canteen and picked up my phone to call Subhash. It was ringing but he wasn't lifting. It rang all the way and the call got cut. My heart started pounding. I was sensing something wrong and bad. I called him again, shaking my thoughts away hoping it was nothing. He didn't lift the call again. I looked at his contact information for a solid 30 seconds not knowing what to do. I called again, pacing from one side to another, thinking about what this could mean. I'm not ready to take anything bad at this point. I'm just not ready to open that box. I want to talk to Subhash immediately. The call got cut again. I gulped the lump in my throat. I dialled him again, pacing fast, feeling desperate by now. When I put the phone to my ear, I stopped walking. I couldn't believe what I was hearing,

The number you are trying to reach is currently switched off.

Switch off? The phone rang before when I called. Did he switch off the phone to avoid me? I stood there like a statue, the phone still stuck to my ear. I felt like I was being pulled down by the earth with double the gravitational force than normal. Just then I heard Akanksha yelling at me,

'Varna. It's chocolates...! A hell lot of them. Sorry, I opened your box.'

I was just staring at the gate. For the first time, the thought of chocolates didn't excite me.

'There is a letter too. Stuck on the inside of the box...'

I turned and ran towards the canteen, pushing Akanksha away. I ran inside and looked at the box. Adi was holding the box.

'Varna. Look at this. This guy must be crazy about you. Look what he did.'

The box had about 50 different varieties of chocolates. One from every brand of chocolate there ever is. I didn't touch even a single one. I pulled the box from Adi and grabbed the letter that was taped on the opening side of the box. I walked out of the canteen and towards the tree where Madhu just gave me this box. I needed privacy and some peace.

Dear Varna,

In the last few months that I have known you, my life has become so much worthier than it ever was. You are an inspiration to me. Your presence made me think, rethink and shape a better future for myself.

Our family have suffered through a tough phase, where we were completely broke when we were in Hyderabad back then. But when my dad shifted to Bangalore to help my uncle with his business, he grew. He made a lot of money and he created value and respect for himself from ground zero. The by-product? Me. I never realized the value of money. I enjoyed having it. I spent a lot of money on unnecessary things and opportunistic friends. The seat in Gitam was bought by my dad with a hell lot of money. I didn't earn it. So, I never knew what my dad had to go through to put me here. I was raised like that and I have been a spoilt brat for a long time. Me being a single kid, they pampered me way too much.

But then, you happened. You were a ray of sunlight in the tunnel of my life. You showed me what life could mean. You showed me the true meaning of happiness and joy. You taught me what it is to be responsible. You have guided me to understand what life is and I have learnt a lot from you like a small kid. Our chats were my school. Our conversations were my lessons. The passion I see in you is my inspiration. You are a celebrity in my life. And all of this without even realizing what you are doing to me.

I wanted to tell you that I got myself together and applied for GRE. I prepared like a maniac and got a good rank. I applied to a few colleges abroad and I got selected into the University of Pennsylvania. I'm going to study MBA there, Varna. I'm going to study hard and make a good career out of it. You remember how you asked me so many questions about what I like, why and everything. I derived my answers from those conversations. I have learnt to follow my heart by looking at you go at your dream. I finally realized what my passion is. It's business Varna. Food business to be clearer. I'm going to finish my MBA and come back to India to start my own business.

So, I guess I'm trying to say... this is it for us. I cannot keep in contact with you while I'm there. And I cannot ask you to wait around for me for another 2-3 years without really knowing what is going to happen. That's not fair. And you are a great catch Varna. Anyone would be lucky to have you. I can't ask you to hold on to me when I'm not sure when I'd return and when I'd start my career. It's just too much to ask.

I would like to say one last thing. I LOVE YOU Varna. With my heart, body, soul and all that I am. I love you now, I loved you for all those years I didn't have you by my side and I loved you even when we were little kids. Even when I didn't know what love really meant. And I will love you for as long as I breathe. You are my angel... My very own personal fairy angel, who came into my life to show me my purpose.

I think I made a little difference in your life too. But I didn't mean to. I'm sorry for that. And I'm sorry for expressing my feelings like this. I couldn't get myself to do this to your face. I'm scared I would fall and crumple and change my mind to go, if I see you in front of me. My heart would be crushed imagining how much I'm going to miss you. But I have to do this. I need to give life a real shot.

Good-Bye...

Forever yours, Subhash.

As I finished the letter, the teardrop that has been waiting on the edge of my eye, jumped out and onto the letter. It fell on his name and I immediately took the hem of my dress and tried to dry it. I looked at the letter, I looked at those three words that I have been waiting to hear and tell and started weeping.

Akanksha must have been looking at me from the canteen window, she came running to me. She sat beside me and hugged me tightly. She rubbed my back lovingly. 'Oh honey...!' she said sympathetically. I wept into her shoulder for several minutes. She just sat there holding me. After what felt like a half hour, I gathered myself and said,

'He left...'

My heart felt heavier than my body. It felt impossible to bare it and it kept becoming heavier every second. I handed the letter to Akanksha. She frowned at me and opened the letter to read it. Another bout of tears just opened up, as she read the letter. I hugged myself tightly. My chest was becoming tighter and my breathing became harder. I felt scared for myself. It was a rather cold day but I was sweating, maybe due to the heat generated in the body for the efforts it made to carry my failing heart. I was hyperventilating by now. I suddenly had a terrible headache. My legs started to hurt too. I didn't know what it was but I thought a little stroll will do me good, so I stood up and walked a few steps. I suddenly felt a pull in my leg, more like a spasm. I started trembling. I looked back at Akanksha to seek help. Before I could reach out to her or call her, I felt the tree, the bench under the tree and Akanksha started to rotate. My entire surroundings turned into a globe and started rotating. Before I realized my body slowly started to bend towards the ground and within a few seconds, my head hit the ground with a big thud.

I heard Akanksha yelling my name and running towards me. My vision began to blur. I tried desperately to open my eyes and look at her. She came to me, pulled me into her lap and started slapping my face. But it didn't hurt. I wasn't feeling any sensation. I heard her yell Adi's name and I tried to turn my head. I saw Aditya running towards me from the canteen. Soon the noises and the blurry visions completely disappeared.

Chapter-7

I opened my eyes to the thermocol ceiling of our university infirmary. I thought I heard my dad talking, so I assumed I might still be dreaming and closed my eyes. But then my mom's gentle loving touch caressed my forehead. Then I opened my eyes completely and looked at the surroundings. My mom helped me wake up from the bed. Everything came back to me. My birthday, the letter, Subhash.... And that he left. I was feeling so confused. I don't know how long ago I fainted, but so much has changed meanwhile. The usual chaotic corridors were silent and dull. I saw Akanksha pacing the corridor with her bag on, outside the infirmary. My mom and dad are here. I saw my dad talking to the physician. I looked at my mom's smiling face. I tried to force a smile at her but I couldn't. I felt way too consumed with sorrow that I didn't have the strength to put up a smile. My dad came towards me holding what looked like a prescription. The physician said,

'Varna. You look better. How are you feeling?'

I nodded with an insincere smile. He smiled back and said,

'You will be all right. Get some rest.'

My dad interfered, 'Thank you, doctor.'

He looked at me and extended his hand. I held onto it and walked with him. Akanksha came towards me, seeing me exit the infirmary. I looked at my dad and said,

'I'll be right behind you Nanna.'

He looked at me and then at Akanksha. Akanksha sensed the worry in his eyes and told him that she would look after me. So, my dad and mom walked out of the college and went straight to the parking lot where our car was parked.

While Akanksha was sitting me down in a chair, I asked her, 'What the hell happened? Why are my parents here? What did you tell them?'

'You had a panic attack, for god's sake! The infirmary was obligated to inform the parents. I didn't tell them anything. But I guess you have to. You do realize that they are going to have questions, right? Are you going to tell them?'

'Did he write when?'

'What?' she asked, confused.

'In the letter. Did he write when he was leaving? He didn't, right?'

'Varna. Stop thinking about the letter.'

'No. Tell me. You have the letter, don't you?'

'Varna... Please. This is not the time you should think and analyse it. Give it some time to settle down in your head.'

'The letter, Akanksha.' I said with a stern voice.

She understood that I was adamant and handed the letter to me from her bag. I opened it and read it again. And again. She saw my temples tighten and my jaw clench. She put her hand on my shoulder and said,

'Varna. Let me hold on to that letter for you. I swear I'll not destroy it. Believe me, I'm so fucking angry that I easily could, but I won't. I respect you and your feelings way too much to do that.'

She slowly tried to pull the letter away from me. I loosened the grip and left it. She folded it and put it back in her bag. She stood up and helped me get to our car. She didn't say anything else. Akanksha knows me well. She knows when and what to talk and when not to. She asked me for my bike keys and signalled that she will drop the bike at my home. I nodded and waved back at her as I passed through the college gates. The whole ride home nobody said a word to me or to each other.

I went into the shower and had a long warm bath and tried to wash the letter off me. I tried not to think of it, but all I could think of was him and the letter. I closed my eyes and lifted my face so that the water directly hit my face. Everything that happened for the last few months flashed in my head. His first message on Orkut, me and Akanksha looking at his picture in her room, me listening to his voice for the first time, the dream of our future, all the silly conversations we had, long phone calls during the nights. And I expected today to be the start of something new, something that I could tell my children and grandchildren about. But it felt like he pulled the carpet harshly from underneath my feet. He took it all away. He made it the end instead of the start.

When I came outside the shower, my mom and dad were sitting in the dining room looking at me. I could feel my eyes double their original size. They swelled up from extensive crying. My nose and chin became cherry red. I knew they had questions. I knew I have to answer them. They deserve to know why their ever-happy and cheery daughter had a panic attack.

'I'll dress up and come. Please serve dinner maa. We shall eat together.'

The plates were set and the food was ready by the time I came in. As I slowly walked towards them and settled in my seat, my mom started talking,

'Honey... Why?'

My dad interfered, 'Let her finish the meal first Geetha.'

'No. I need to know. I have waited long enough.' My mom was becoming restless. 'What is it Varna? You seemed genuinely happy in the morning. Or were you pretending? Is something wrong Sweetie? Are you taking pressure on your grades or something? Or is it the college?'

These are the people who trusted me and believed in me. It felt ridiculous to tell them all of this happened because I fell in love with a guy. But I couldn't avoid it. I couldn't lie to them either.

'It's a boy, maa.'

'What? Who is it? What happened? Did someone abuse you? Did someone force themselves on to you?'

'Geetha...!' my dad yelled at my mom. We both gasped. He probably couldn't bare if any of them were true. Or maybe he was so sure that I could handle such things that they can't bring me to a 'panic attack' level.

'No! Maa. I'm not harmed. I'm absolutely fine. This boy is not from my college. Not even from this city. And soon, not even from the country. You don't need to worry about him anymore. This won't happen again. I promise. I'm sorry I put you guys through this.'

'Sorry!? No. You don't need to be. As parents, we are just concerned about your well-being. That is all.'

'If you say this won't happen again, I'll believe you Kanna. But if it does or you see any symptoms of it happening again, please know that you can talk to us. We might not be able to help you with the issue but we can surely protect you from anything in this world. You have to know that you have very supportive parents at home.' my dad declared.

I looked at both of them, smiling, feeling extremely grateful. 'I know Nanna.'

I took my mom's hand and squeezed it to reassure her that I was fine. She smiled back and we had a good dinner. My mom and dad came into my room to get me to sleep. I told them I'd be fine but they were adamant. My mom started gently tapping on me singing a lullaby that I used to sleep to when I was a baby. My dad just sat across the room in darkness. I felt embarrassed. I should have contained myself better. I should have reacted to the whole thing in a different way. Probably because of the crying and being tired or because of my mom's lullaby I fell asleep quite quickly.

I woke up early the next morning to see my mom sleeping in my room on the floor. I cribbed and woke her up.

'What is it, honey? Are you okay?'

'I'm okay maa. It's morning. Wake up. Why did you sleep here? I told you I was fine. You didn't need to.'

'No. It's not really for you Kanna. I couldn't sleep last night.'

'Maa, as I promised yesterday, never again. Okay? I have it under control.'

We both went and freshened up. I helped her around the kitchen to pack lunches for my dad and me. I helped her serve the breakfast. My dad seemed pleasantly surprised to see me doing better.

'You look well Varna.'

'I am, Nanna. I'm fine.'

'Anyway, let's go.' He said picking up his keys.

'Let's go? Akanksha didn't get my bike last night?'

'She did. But I feel like dropping you off today. Would you allow me the honour?'

He said dramatically.

'Nanna. If this is about what happened yesterday...'

He cut me mid-sentence and said, 'Absolutely not. I know you said you are dealing with it. I trust you madam. I just want to drop and pick you up from college today.'

I agreed and went along. On the way to the college, I zoned out. I wasn't thinking about anything in particular. I was probably analysing how low I was feeling and how extensively Subhash affected me by leaving me hanging like this. Akanksha was waiting near the college entrance by the time I reached college. My dad dropped me at the gate seeing Akanksha there. He waved at me and left.

'How are you doing Varna?' she asked as we started walking towards the campus.

'I don't know.' I said observing some students looking at me strangely. 'So how many people saw the fiasco yesterday?'

'Quite a lot.' She said. 'You fainted dude.'

'Damn it. This is so embarrassing. What do they know?'

'Nobody knows anything about the letter. Except, well, Aditya.' I looked at her with a frown.

'What can I say? He was with me all the time. He's a very caring and helpful guy. He was the one who lifted you and carried you to the infirmary. He was the one that drove me home on your bike last night. He said he would drop it off at your place.'

'Oh, my god. Carried me? Literally?'

'Yes. How did you think you ended up in the infirmary?'

'Wow. My feelings for him, all the fantasies, all those feelings, and finally when he touches me and lifts me, I'm unconscious.' I laughed at the irony. Akanksha didn't seem to enjoy the joke. She put a straight face and turned away.

'You are scaring me Varna. Yesterday you were so upset that you cried like a baby and had a panic attack. Today you act like nothing happened at all. Both the reactions are a little extreme.'

My smile faded away.

'Akanksha. Subhash doesn't exist in my life anymore. He never did and he never will. I was an idiot to create this imaginary vision of something that was not even there. I was stupid enough to let him affect me so much that I worry the people I love the most. My mom and dad are here. You are here. Aditya is here. You guys care a lot about me and I'm not going to make you all see me walk through hell. I'm fine. Even if I'm not, I will be with time. Okay?'

'See. This is what I'm talking about. The extreme reactions. You don't need to hide your real emotions and put on a fake smile and pretend just because we care for you! It's okay to feel bad. I understand that you feel devastated. Talk about it. Or maybe confront him. You have his phone number. Get a fucking closure. He doesn't deserve you Varna. End this chapter.'

'Look, I understand if you hate him for what he did. But I still love him. I don't want closure. I don't want to confront him. It's all confusing and new to me. I need to figure out what I should do. Until then I'm staying put.'

She rolled her eyes and muttered under her breath, 'Unbelievable!'

I understand her. She is the one person who knows every single thing that has happened between me and him. She is the one who has seen me from 0 to 100 in the process of falling madly in love, obsessing over him and now losing him again. Her intentions and suggestions are valid but I can't do that. I'm not ready to accept that he just left. I can't think about the what and why of it all. I'm determined to be cool and more present and make sure that I'm okay and ready to deal with Subhash.

Chapter - 8

It has been almost three months since my birthday and that horrific incident. Even though I was trying to look and feel better, I wasn't successful. I haven't been eating well, sleeping well or even studying well. Akanksha was really upset with me. My mom and dad were worried about me. They were taking me to the movies, brought my favourite foods, and the other day we all went out shopping. But it's not working. I'm genuinely trying to smile more and be more present but I'm consumed with the thoughts of Subhash. I see him everywhere I go and I feel his presence. I feel like nothing of this happened at all and I didn't see the letter and I'm still hoping to see him again. I kept messaging him on Orkut. I kept calling his phone number. He has been avoiding me. Today my dad booked tickets for '*Yeto Vellipoyindi Manasu*' my favourite actor Nani's film. As I was getting ready my dad yelled from the living room,

'We will miss the titles. You know how I hate to miss even a single second of the screening...! Come on out, Varna.'

I looked at myself in the mirror and tried to smile but instead, I just dropped my shoulders as I remembered how Subhash promised me to be here by now and watch this movie together. I let out a deep breath and walked out. My mom saw me and said,

'Wow, Kanna. You look like an angel.'

Angel... My own personal angel. He said that in the letter. I swallowed the huge lump that formed in my throat and told myself that I wouldn't ruin this day. I walked along with them and we went to the theatre.

It was interval time. For a few minutes, I forgot what was going on with me and completely fell in love with Nani's performance. I was so happy; I was discussing the first half with my mom and my dad started guessing what could happen in the second half.

Just then I saw Subhash pass through the stairs from beside us. I frowned and my eyes followed him. My smile vanished and my whole demeanour changed. I felt all the pain that I felt in the last few days. I felt betrayed. I felt every single emotion related to sorrow. My dad, who was sitting on the aisle seat, saw me changing and shook me. He asked,

'What is it Kanna? What happened?'

I whispered to myself *Is that him?* My dad asked again, 'What is it?'

I immediately jumped up from my seat and started running towards the exit from where he left. I ran outside and scanned the area for a second. I saw him walking towards the washroom and proceeded that way. I was determined to confront him now. He entered the men's washroom. I didn't care. I kept walking in that direction. Just then my dad came behind me and held me tightly. I was not in a position to realize what was happening. I kept pushing him away and tried to get inside the washroom. My dad kept whispering in my ears.

'Kanna please relax. That's the men's washroom.' But I didn't care. I kept pushing him away saying, 'Leave me. It's him. I need to see him.' I yelled his name out 'Subhash...!'

The people around us kept staring. Everyone became silent, left what they were doing and stared at this stupid girl who was yelling that she wants to go into the men's restroom and her dad holding her tight and controlling her. My dad's grip was strong so I couldn't move anymore. Just then he exited the washroom. I immediately stopped moving. I became so still and looked at him with disappointment. My dad slowly released me. I saw the guy whom I thought was Subhash. He looked very similar to him. He was tall, fair and broad-shouldered. But it wasn't Subhash. He looked at me, confused and walked away. I realized what just happened and felt awkward. I was about to lose control over my body and drop down, but my dad held me and pulled me towards a seat. He sat me down and didn't leave me. Everything came back to me. I realized how much I was missing Subhash and how desperately I want to see him and beg him not to leave me. But I couldn't do that. He never even gave me a chance. He just left. He broke up with me over a letter...! That letter came in front of my eyes. I closed my tightly and covered my face trying to stop that thing from being seen. I cried into my palms. My dad just sat beside me rubbing my arm.

People slowly began to vanish as the show started again. Just then my mom came out searching for us. She was looking around and when she finally saw us, she smiled at my dad and came to us. As she came closer, she observed that I was crying and came running to me and sat beside me.

'Varna... what is it...!?'

My dad looked at my mom and signalled that he will update her later. She nodded and said,

'Let's go Kanna. Doesn't matter if we miss the second half. Let's go home.'

I inhaled sharply and wiped my face. I shook my head and said,

'I'm sorry. I overreacted to something. I'm fine. Let's go back inside. I want to watch what will happen next. Come on.'

I stood up and started walking but they both just sat there and stared at me, sympathetically. I looked back and said,

'Come on...! We all know how Varna's love story ended. We don't want to miss knowing what happened to Varun and Nitya now, do we?'

They stood up and walked slowly behind me. We finished the movie and went home. Mom and Dad didn't understand what to talk to me. I was feeling bad to have to put them through this. After coming home, my dad parked the car and asked my mom to get his bike keys. She looked at me, confused. I looked at my dad. He said, 'I'm going to take you out for some ice cream. Is that okay?'

I smiled and nodded. We rode to the Necklace Road, bought Cornetto cones and found ourselves a bench to sit on. I happily started to indulge in my ice cream and my dad started talking,

'So… It's the same guy, huh? Subhash?'

'Nanna?'

'I remember how lonely you felt and how long it took for you to make friends again when their family left for Bangalore. So? Tell me. Is it the same guy?'

'Nanna… It's not like that.'

'Is it him, Varna?'

'Yes. I told Mom a few months ago that he texted me on Orkut. We connected and…' I hesitated.

'Yes?'

'It's not his fault Nanna. I'm the one who fell in love. I'm the one who assumed we would be together. I'm the one who thought he would come and surprise me on my birthday. It's on me.'

He nodded and started having his ice cream. I looked at my dad, feeling guilty. He looked back and signalled for me to have my ice cream. I slowly finished my cone dwelling in his thoughts. My dad started talking,

'What exactly happened on your birthday Varna?'

I gulped and began talking. I told him everything about our relationship progress. How we talked over the phone and how I assumed he would come to Hyderabad and surprise me but instead sent his friend Madhu to deliver the letter and the gift box. I briefly told him the contents of the letter too.

'So... He is going to the States to pursue MBA. How is that a reason to break up with you? Are you sure it's just that? Or maybe he was with someone else all along...'

I cut him mid-sentence, 'No... No way, Nanna. I love him and he loves me. He mentioned that in the letter too. He finally told me that he loves me but... I don't know, not living in the same country and not having the time or the sources to call or text each other whenever we want might be the reason he left. And somehow, he thought I would be stupid enough to forget him and find myself some other guy by the time he returns.'

My dad nodded trying to understand the whole thing. He said, 'You know... When me and Amma decided to get married, it took us 2 months to tell our parents. We just finished college and we were at home not having a source to communicate. We decided we would meet each other at a particular place on a specific day and time. I told *Bamma* first. She readily agreed. It took a little while for *Thatha* to come to terms though.'

'Really?' I asked excited to hear their story.

'When we were finally meeting at that place, I was so excited to tell her that my parents agreed and I wanted to hear what her parents had to say. Amma came, looking all worried and tensed. When I asked her what happened, she said she could not get herself to tell her father about us.'

I laughed and said, 'Typical Amma.'

'Yeah. I tried to convince her in multiple ways and gave her multiple ideas on how to break the news to him but she got so scared that she just burst out crying, imagining she had to do this. So finally, I had to convince *Thatha* to go and talk to her dad. That's how our match became an arranged marriage.'

'Haha. It's crazy how she claims that hers was a love marriage.'

'It is…! We loved each other enough to take that risk… Kanna. There is a whole world for you to explore out there. Your ambition to start your own business. You have so much to do with your life. Look, I'm not saying you need to forget about this guy. But don't ruin your precious life for what doesn't even seem like a relationship.

'Nanna…'

'I know you love him with all your heart. I see that. But you can't force the other person to stay in love now, can you? Just keep your mind and heart open. Let it heal. Let it find love again. You deserve that Varna.'

I just zoned out repeating his words in my head. I started thinking about Subhash. I questioned myself if he was worth the wait. But every question had just one answer. I love him more than he can even imagine. Maybe I should have been the one to propose first. He would have understood my love and reciprocated it.

My dad pulled me out of my trance. As we walked towards our bike, he put his arm around me. I looked at him and smiled. Just as we were about to start back home, I called out to my dad and said,

'Nanna. Please don't tell Amma that it's Subhash. It might ruin her opinion of him and also her friendship with Kavitha Aunty.'

'Of course, madam. I understand. Your secret is safe with me.'

Chapter-9

POV - Akanksha

Everybody was gathered around the bulletin board and I pushed myself through the crowd to check our grades for the semester. I walked back with a dropped face towards the canteen where Adi and Varna were seated. They were laughing, probably at a joke Adi made. He has the most amazing and non-offensive sense of humour ever. Adi observed me and stopped laughing and frowned at me.

'Akshu... What's the matter?'

Varna was still smiling. I didn't know how to break it to her. She didn't fail but she has scored drastically less than the last semester which is not like her at all.

'You got 89%. And Varna.... 67%. I'm sorry.'

'What... You're joking right?' she said.

I let out a tired sigh and shook my head. She ran towards the results board. I looked at her and cribbed.

'I'm really worried about her Adi. It's almost been a year. I know for a fact that she is still not over him. Now it affected her grades too.'

'You worry too much Akshu.' He bent forward and pulled my chair closer to his, an action which caught me off guard. 'Look, you have done everything in your power and strength to make her feel better, did you not?'

My heart was pounding. His face was so close to mine, I could almost smell his misty scent. I was lost looking deeply into his eyes that I didn't even hear what he just said. I just nodded. He sat straight and said, 'Then? What else can you do?'

I just turned towards the table and sipped at the coffee that he ordered for me. Adi and I have been friends for quite a while now. But I developed feelings towards him ever since that night of Varna's big fiasco. He has been so considerate and caring. Ironically, I guess I fell for him when I saw him lifting Varna and carrying her to the infirmary. That day I didn't see a goofball, funny guy that happens to be our friend. I saw an extremely caring person who values friendship a lot. He felt Varna would be embarrassed if he or anyone else except me was around, so he waited for me in the classroom. After I sent Varna home, I ran to the classroom. There he was, alone, waiting for me. The first thing he asked me was how I was doing. Because he knew how much Varna meant to me. With so much focus being on Varna, he cared enough to ask me that question. He walked with me towards Varna's bike and offered to drive me.

Ever since that day, my days and nights have been consumed with Adi's thoughts. I think about him more than ever. I observe him and understand him more than ever. I don't know if this is love. I wanted to talk to Varna about the whole thing, but she was going through so much and I wasn't sure how she'd react if I told her I had feelings for her crush.

Adi shook me from my trance and said, 'Hello Ms. Daydreamer...! Class is about to begin. Let's go.' I packed my things and left for class thinking about Varna and how is she going to handle her grades.

By the time I entered the class, Varna was already there with her textbook open. I went, sat beside her and asked if she was okay. She nodded and immersed herself in the book again. After the classes, I asked her to come to my place so we could spend some time but she didn't. She left. That evening I got a call from her father...

'Hello, uncle. Please tell me.'

'Hi, Akanksha. How are you doing?'

'I'm fine uncle...' I didn't know if he knew about the results.

'Okay... So, Varna came home and went straight into her room. She isn't talking to anyone. Did something happen today?'

'Uncle. Last semester's results came out and she scored a little less. Maybe she is upset about that. Other than that, she is fine.'

'Ohhh... Is it? She is fine you say?'

'Yes, uncle. Absolutely. She has been smiling and laughing a lot more. She is trying to get over him.'

'That's great news maa. Thank you so much and I'm sorry again, to be troubling you like this.'

'No, I understand, uncle.'

'You are very sweet maa. God bless you. Bye then.'

I inhaled deeply and sat on my bed. Prakash Uncle has been calling me now and then for the last few months to find out if Varna was doing okay in college. The first time he called, he told me how she thought someone was Subhash and almost followed him into the restroom. I was so shocked to hear that. For the first few months, she was very serious, she didn't talk to anyone, she wouldn't even lift her head. She would come straight into the classroom and leave straight home after the classes. I feel it was Aditya who got her out of her zone every time. He would crack some silly joke and she would smile. And slowly over the last few months that smile turned into laughter. She hasn't been coming home as often as she used to, ever since that day. She prefers to just be at home. And in college, Adi has always been around, even if I had to talk to her about Subhash. I doubt if she is developing feelings for Adi in the hope to move on from Subhash.

She has closed herself so much that I genuinely have no clue what is going on in her head. What if she is considering Adi? She always liked him. And he was a great tool to help her cope with Subhash. I don't know if she is over him at all. I tried a couple of times to talk about Subhash but then she would instantly close up like a touch-me-not plant. She wouldn't talk to me about anything else too that whole day. Is she embarrassed by what happened? Is she trying to completely cut him off of her life or is she secretly still in love with that ass****. She knows I'll be mad at her if she tells me she has forgiven him and wants to make contact with him. The first time we all downloaded WhatsApp on our phones a few months ago, she was weirdly very happy. She said something like, 'So we can contact anyone, anywhere and not count the number of messages sent in a day or think about data roaming or stuff like that right?'. I asked what she meant by *anyone, anywhere* and *roaming charges*. She completely ignored my question and when asked if she meant Subhash, she fell silent. She might have thought of contacting him but that guy never even left her a number. Never gave her a chance to respond to his stupid letter.

While I was immersed in thoughts, I heard Aditya's bike horn thrice, our code for him to let me know he has arrived. I immediately ran towards my window and slid the curtain away. There he was, waiting for me with badminton rackets on his back. He waved at me and showed his watch, signalling me to come down. We made a new habit to go to the new Badminton court that they built in our community at least thrice a week. It was a walkable distance from my house but a little far from Adi's. I saw him on the street once, going there with his friend and asked him about it the next day in college. A few weeks later he asked if I was interested to join him since his friend moved to another apartment further away. I readily agreed considering my love for badminton too and also, we played multiple games at our apartments many times before. It's been almost two months and we never missed our schedule. As my house was right on the way to the court, he waits for me downstairs and we go together.

As I exited the elevator and walked towards him, he kept staring at me like something was wrong. I frowned. He asked,

'You look dull. What happened?'

'Hmmm, nothing. Varna's dad called.' I said and sat on his bike. He started driving and kept talking,

'So? How is she doing?'

'She looked upset, he said. Didn't talk to them too.'

'Poor girl. Such a bright soul she was. I hope she slowly begins to recover. Subhash is old news now.'

'Yeah.' I said and got off the bike as we arrived at the court. We went inside and the court was a full house that day. When we went to the reception, they said there was one court open for a Doubles game, where there was another couple already playing. I felt a little hesitant but Adi seemed happy. He said 'Yayyy' dramatically and high-fived. I looked at him doubtfully but followed him. We have played opposite each other but never played on the same team. He is a great sport. Win or lose, he appreciated the game and always encouraged me. After the game, we discussed mine and his best moves while we packed our bags. But being on the same team as him, suddenly put me under pressure. I didn't want to let him down.

After almost an hour and a very hectic game, we won by a very slight margin. It was a great game though. As we were wiping our sweat and packing our bags, Adi bent towards me and said, 'Would you like to have some juice or something? Winning treat. I'll pay.'

I agreed and we both went to the nearest juice centre. I ordered *Mausambi* juice and he ordered sapota juice to be fancy. After we got our order Adi took a sip and instantly hated it. I sipped mine and began to enjoy it, making yummy sounds just to rub it in his face. He got annoyed and what he did next startled me. He took his straw and put it into my juice and started sipping, while my straw was still in my mouth. I gasped and moved back. For a second it felt like we were sharing a kiss or maybe it was my hormones just exaggerating the situation. I looked at him, defeated and handed over the glass to him and took his juice. I don't know if he did it consciously, but he took the straw he was drinking and put it in the sapota juice in my hand. He was happily sipping my juice now, looking at the traffic and slightly rocking his body, like nothing happened. I looked at him lovingly, slowly realizing that I was falling in love with him. The way back home was torturous for me. I desperately wanted to take away the badminton rackets that were between us and hug him tightly. He dropped me home and without looking back, waved his hand and went away. I kept looking at him till he crossed our street.

The next day when I entered college and saw Varna's bike already there, I smiled to myself and went to the classroom. She was reading a book. Strangely it wasn't a textbook. She was reading a book that I gifted her a few months ago to cope with her situation, *You Are a Badass* by *Jan Sincero*. When she saw me near her, she lifted her head and greeted me with a broad smile. She has been smiling more often than not these days, but I know when she smiles from her heart and when from her lips. This was a heartful smile and that made me extremely happy.

'Hey, Akanksha. I have been waiting for you. I texted you on WhatsApp that I'll be early today. Haven't you checked?'

'No. I'm sorry. What is it?'

'Nothing. Just wanted to spend some extra time with you. It's been a while, isn't it? Just you and me?'

'Yeah…! I'm glad you recognise that.'

'I also wanted to tell you something.'

'Umhmm… I'm listening.'

'I'm sorry… Akanksha. I have been avoiding you.'

I didn't see that coming. At least not today. I imagined the semester results would put her into a box again but she seems surprisingly upbeat and she is apologising for lost time.

'Say something please.'

'Varna. I don't want you to be sorry.' I said, placing an arm around her. 'My only true wish is that you don't lose your original self. You are too precious to lose yourself for someone like Subhash.'

She took a deep breath and bent her head down. I guess she still isn't okay with me being rude about him. 'Look Varna. I'm happy you are realizing it. And you know that I'll be here for you right? Whatever it is.'

'Yes'. There was that lovely smile again. The day went very pleasantly. Varna was beginning to look and feel more like herself. She was cracking jokes, talking about study topics as passionately as she did before. At the end of the day after all the classes she said,

'Akanksha, I believe we should start our combined study sessions. That would help me with my grades and my personal life. Is that okay?'

I loved the idea at first. I loved the thought of having my best friend back again and talking to her, studying with her, and watching movies with her was my favourite thing to do. But suddenly it dawned upon me that I'd have to miss a few badminton sessions with Adi. My face fell and I guess she observed that.

'What is it, dude?'

I shook the thought off and told myself that Varna needs me now.

'It's nothing Varna. Let's go. What about we buy Cornetto on the way home and watch a few episodes of *Friends* first?'

'Ooh, awesome...!! let's do that.'

She is as crazy a *Friends* show fan as I am. *Friends* was one of the many things that we bonded over in the beginning. We would constantly take *Friends* references in our conversations and we referred to each other as Monica and Rachel. I guess me more than her. Friends is my go-to safe place. I even recommended watching episodes of Friends when Varna was in a bad place, but it didn't work on her.

That evening when we were studying, I heard Adi's bike horn. I didn't inform him about my study session with Varna. I ran up to the window and saw him waiting for me. He looked at me with a smile and waved at me. At that exact moment, I felt like leaving everything behind, not caring about anything or anyone and just running quickly into his arms. My body was heating up with new sensations. Just then Varna's hand on my shoulder interrupted my thoughts. She looked and exclaimed, 'Hey! Adi is here? Awesome. Did you invite him?'

'No. You wait here. Let me go talk to him.' I said and walked out of the room before she could react. I ran downstairs. He was looking at me doubtfully as I was not dressed for our game.

'Akshu... Don't tell me you are not coming.'

'Adi. I'm sorry. Varna is here. We are studying.'

'Ohhh... How is she? Hasn't it been a while since she came here? What's the deal?'

'Well, the results, the other day. They got to her. She decided to turn her life around and be more... herself. So, we decided to start our group study sessions.' I said feeling a little disappointed.

'All right. Then what about Badminton?'

'We won't do this every day though. I will let you know when I'm free.'

He looked away, dropping his shoulders very evidently. That brought a smile to my face. I asked, 'What is it?'

He looked at me, shook his head and started his bike. 'It's nothing. I'm just glad she is back.' He said turning his bike back towards his apartment.

'So, you are not going either?' I asked curiously. He turned back and looked at me with a smile for about 4 seconds.

'It's not as much fun with anyone else.' He said.

That brought a very huge smile to my face. Or I guess I was blushing.

I entered my room still blushing as my smile refused to come back. Varna was standing at the window staring outside. I inhaled sharply and said,

'So, shall we continue?'

'What was that all about?' she asked still facing outside the window.

'Oh, nothing. He was just asking about you. I told him we are back with our sessions. And he says he is happy for you.'

I was looking intensely at her waiting for her response. I was hoping she would ask more, so I can jump in and tell her everything about what's happening with me related to Aditya. I was beginning to become desperate to share this feeling. I want to confess, say it out loud and make it real. But I saw her smiling when she turned back. I frowned and asked her what was the matter.

'I don't know. Don't you think it's very sweet that he still cares a lot about me?'

I was very disappointed with her reaction. How can she not see it? Adi came to my house, willing to talk to me! Not her. But I couldn't say anything. As much as I'm interested in Adi, as much as I hate her for this ignorance, I still care a great deal about her. I saw her go through everything that I'm going through right now with Subhash. I saw how devastated she was when he left. And she became an entirely different person for a whole year. And as her friend, it's my responsibility to help her build herself back.

'He is generally a very caring guy Varna.' I replied and cut off the topic entirely. We continued our studies for another hour or so and she left home.

That night I couldn't sleep for quite some time. I kept rolling around the bed. This whole situation with my best friend who might be interested in my other best friend whom I want to make my boyfriend, who I'm not sure if he likes me at all. I wanted to talk to someone. I wanted to release some tension. I woke up and started pacing the room. I walked towards the window and moved the curtain away. I kept staring at the spot where Adi always comes and waits for me. I could feel him. His bike, the sound of its horn, the excitement my heart feels when I see him. I decided to call Srikar.

Srikar has been our friend for a very little time but we connected well. But during the summer holidays last year, he picked up a new habit from his neighbour who was also a senior in our college. When he smokes, he hangs out with this other gang behind the canteen. In the beginning, Adi was a little upset that Srikar was changing too much and was worried for him. I believe he even talked to him a couple of times about how smoking is not good for his health. But Srikar was adamant and ignored Adi. So slowly we have drifted apart. Varna was in her own world anyway. So, Adi and I grew a lot closer. We discovered a lot of things that we have in common. I definitely can't talk about it to Varna. But Srikar could help me. I got cut off from the thoughts that were going on in my head when he finally picked up the call.

'Hey, Akanksha. What's up? Is everything okay?'

'Hey Yeah. Everything is fine. Is this a good time to talk? Are you even awake?'

'Yeah of course. Anytime for you. I'm with a friend, just chilling.'

Probably smoking, I assumed.

'Hmmm... Sri. There has been so much happening around me that I can't talk to anyone else. I'm feeling so lost.'

'Wait a minute. Let me step aside....' Silence for a minute. 'Akanksha hey. So, is this about Adi?'

'What?' I was shocked he guessed it right away. 'What do you mean?'

'I mean. I'm pretty sure something is happening between you and Adi. Half the class knows it. Many assume that you are in a relationship!'

I enjoyed the thought of people assuming we are in a relationship. Is it that evident? Or maybe people just thought we look great together or maybe it's because of how well we get along.

'Akanksha... I'm sorry. I spoke too soon. Please tell me.'

'It is about Adi...' I hesitated. '...I guess......' I couldn't finish the statement. This would be the first time I would have said it aloud. I remember how Varna was blushing when she confessed to me about Subhash. I remember her smile, her heartful, soulful smile. Strangely and sadly, I didn't have the same smile. 'It's nothing, Sri. I'm sorry to have disturbed you.' I said and cut the call. I regretted calling him at all. He immediately called me back.

'Akanksha, listen. I understand that you are hesitant. I know I'm not your best friend, Varna is and maybe Adi. So, I understood when you called me that you need advice on something related to them. Don't forget that I'm your friend too! Talk to me.' I was silent for a bit but continued to talk.

'I guess I'm in love with Adi.' I declared.

'Wow! That's awesome. Adi would be thrilled to hear that. Believe me!'

'Why would you say that? Did he say something to you?'

'No. Not really. But I can guess. So, what's the issue? You wanted to find out if he'd be interested. You want me to play cupid?' He said sounding excited.

'The issue... is... I guess Varna loves him too.'

'What...!!!???' He screamed. 'How do you guess? Tell me what happened exactly?'

'Nothing specifically. She is just now slowly recovering from that blow last year. I believe the reason to be Adi. She has been smiling a lot around him, talking about him, asking about him. And she was the one who first had a crush on Adi for almost the first two years of college.'

'So? Why don't you just ask her? Or rather tell her that you like him. You are better suited to Adi than anyone else I know. I mean Varna is great but... You know what I mean.' he said. That made my heart pump an extra litre of fresh blood.

'I can't though. What if she is interested in him? I can't see her heart break again.'

'So!? Instead, you will break yours? What kind of a sacrifice is that? Are you crazy?' My eyes welled up a little and I gulped.

'I don't know Sri. I'm confused.'

'Look, Akanksha. You are looking too much into this. Varna is a great friend and an amazing person. The whole class liked her. But then she gave her heart to Subhash! And when he left, she became so self-centred, ignorant and lost. How long did you try? A year? Or more? Did she change? No. She broke many rules of friendship too if you ask me. Do you want to give up your soulmate for her?' As much as I was liking the angle, I hated that he spoke about Varna like that. She was, is and will be my best friend forever. What we have is something that maybe Srikar can never understand.

'Are you the one talking about breaking the rules of friendship? Really?'

That probably hit him. He didn't say a word for the next 10 seconds. I let it sink in. I got really mad that he thought he could bad mouth Varna to me!

'...I understand I have been a little distant. I'm sorry yaar.'

'Not to me. Adi worries a lot about you Sri. You were his only friend.'

'Hmmm... Okay. Anyway, about that, I think you should confess to Adi. You'll know what he has in his mind right? And according to Adi's response, you can slowly let Varna know. And I guess she will be happy that you have found love. Varna is a mature girl. She only had a crush on Adi, she didn't love him. I don't think she loved anyone as much as she loved that guy anyway. That was intense.' I thought that was great advice.

'Okay... Thank you, Sri. And I'm sorry about what I said before.'

'No. That's okay. I'm realizing it too. I didn't do very well this semester. There is just one semester left to complete the course, I can't fool around anymore. I get that. I will talk to Adi too. Thank you.'

'Okay. Good for you! Bye, Srikar.'

I cut the call and the time flashed on the screen. It was 2:15 am. I rolled my eyes and crawled into my bed, throwing my phone away. I felt a kind of weight put aside from my shoulders. It sounded easy. Tell Adi, depending on his reaction, tell Varna. I was pretty clear by now what should be my next course of action. But one thing Srikar said caught my attention. *I don't think she loved anyone as much as she loved that guy anyway. That was intense.* It was very intense. I remembered the conversation we once had when I asked her whether she loved Adi as she loved Subhash. I remember how offensive she felt when I compared them both. Maybe that is still the mindset she is in. Maybe Adi was just that for her, a crush, that she had gotten over when Subhash happened. Maybe talking to her will solve all my problems. But yeah, before I could tell her I need to see where Adi is. I went to sleep and determined that tomorrow will be the day I will tell Aditya about my feelings.

The next morning, I woke up, freshened up and had my breakfast. I tried multiple outfits but decided to go with casual. I picked a comfortable white crop top with a high waist blue jegging and paired them with sneakers. I left my hair open and left for college. That day, unfortunately, my bus got delayed and I reached college just a few minutes after the first class has already started. I was still panting when I entered the class and sat beside Varna. She smiled at me and said, 'You look cool today.'

I mouthed *Thank you* at Varna and scanned the classroom for Adi. I found him towards the back of the class, writing something in his notebook and just then lifted his head to look at the professor. He observed me staring at him and raised his eyebrows and waved at me with a broad smile. I smiled back at him and turned towards the front. I took a deep breath and told myself, *That's it. He is the one and today is the day!*

During the lunch break, we all headed to the canteen. I was walking slowly thinking about how to start a conversation about it, should I ask him to come out or maybe I should just talk to him while going home? Me, Varna and Adi sat at our regular table but we were surprised by an unexpected visitor, Srikar.

'Hey, Srikar. Long time no see. How are you doing?' asked Varna.

Adi's face was blank. He hadn't talked much to Srikar after the last time he got annoyed about Adi's nagging about smoking.

'What do you mean? You see me every day. I see you every day.'

'Yeah, but not as before right... Anyway, how did you score in the mids?'

'Just fine. I passed. So, tell me about your situation. How's your boyfriend Subhash?' He said teasingly. Me and Adi jumped up in our seats and looked at each other with wide eyes. I don't know if he got offended because she asked about his grades or if he is asking this regarding our conversation last night. I felt a chill in my spine and I interrupted.

'Sri...!? What's wrong with you? Are you high or something?'

'No. I'm not. But I know someone who is...! It's none other than our dear friend Varna here!' He started laughing. 'High on life. High on Subhash... Did he come back to you yet?' Varna's expression was changing. She isn't laughing anymore. I saw her jaw clenching. And Srikar was high and way out of control. I glared at Adi, signalling him to do something. Varna was looking pretty cold, frozen, almost deathly. Srikar was still laughing like a mad guy when Adi lifted him holding his arm and started dragging him out of the canteen. Srikar pushed him away and looked back at Varna from a distance.

'Varna. I'm sorry if I said something wrong. Don't you think they are overreacting? I was just casually asking...' He said, almost pausing mid-sentence and looking around him. We were towards the far end of the canteen and Sri and Adi were almost towards the entrance of the canteen and everyone in between suddenly fell silent and started staring at us. Adi didn't want Sri to make a bigger scene of it so he started pushing him out. I was right beside her holding her arm. She pushed my hand away and started to speak.

'You know what Sri... Subhash was never even my boyfriend. It's been a year since he left and I couldn't care any less.'

'Oh really? So, you are saying you are single and ready to mingle?

'Absolutely! In fact...' she paused and started walking towards them. There was something different about her body language. Rude, arrogant, a bit of carelessness, definitely not like her. She went dangerously close to Srikar, so close I guessed she could have smelled if he was high! *What was she planning?* I began to worry. She looked into his eyes for a few seconds and suddenly turned towards Aditya and said,

'Adi... Would you like to go out on a date with me?' She asked.

Thud... I felt a huge rock, literally the size of that room, fall on my heart. My body felt so heavy that I dropped onto the chair behind me. Adi immediately looked at me. Srikar was shocked too. He was staring at me, Varna and then Adi. The whole canteen almost gasped at once. Adi kept staring at me probably not knowing what to answer. Does he want to say yes? I guess he might have observed the teardrops formed in my eyes. He has mastered the art of reading me so well in the past few months.

'So? What is it, Adi?' Varna said. Her voice sounded vulnerable for a second. But when Adi didn't answer she looked back at me and then at him and said, 'Okay then. We'll go to *Waterfront*, Necklace Road. Pick me up at 8 o'clock.' She said and walked out of the canteen. Adi who was still holding Srikar's arm pushed him away with force and sprinted towards me. Srikar didn't expect the events to turn out this way. He came and sat at the table. I was still frozen. My heart ached so bad that my throat gave up functioning.

'Akshu... What the hell just happened? Did you know anything about this?'

'Akanksha I'm so sorry. I didn't expect her to react that way. Even if she did, why Adi? Why not... I don't know, anyone else. Me maybe? What was that?'

I looked at Srikar with a deathly glare. He shut his mouth immediately and stood up to go out as the bell rang. He went behind Adi and mouthed *Tell him now*. I rolled my eyes and looked out the window. After almost everyone left, Adi pulled his stool towards mine and sat in front of me. He put one of his hands on my thigh and tried to pull my face to face him with the other. Everything that I was feeling suddenly felt so little compared to what his touch just did to me. He was still holding on to my jaw. I controlled my emotions and looked at him.

'Listen. I have been wanting to tell you something for a while now. I like...' I immediately closed his mouth with my hand, shocking myself. He was startled. He stared into my eyes, not saying anything. That stare pierced through my eyes and went directly to my heart. It didn't stop there but travelled to a much farther place down south. We both shook off and sat straight.

'I think you should go, Adi.' I said with a straight face. He frowned immediately.

'What the hell...!?' He said. I interrupted him again.

'Look. Whatever it is that is going on here... cannot happen Adi. Varna had a crush on you since the first day of college. Almost for three and half years now. You helped her like an anchor when she was falling apart. She needs you now more than ever. I hope you understand.'

His frown never went off. He was looking at me with a hint of anger. I couldn't imagine what he was feeling. I didn't want to. At this point, I only want Varna to get back to herself. And if a date or maybe a relationship with Adi helps her get there, that is exactly what I should help her with. I stood up and walked past him. He sat there not moving his vision. He was still angrily staring at the chair I was sitting on when I saw him just before I left the canteen.

Chapter-10

POV- Varna

I wore the best and most fancy outfit I own and got ready for our date. 'I thought you said you were going out with your friends...?' My mom asked doubtfully looking at me from top to bottom.

'Yes, I am, Amma.' I said nonchalantly.

'Okay... You look good. To be honest, a little overdressed. Anyway, who is coming?' She inquired. I rolled my eyes at her and looked back at the mirror. I am overdressed but that's okay... Date night or a friend's hangout night, it's been quite a while since I have been out at all, including study sessions with Akanksha. I know my mom was suspecting something. Being her curious self, of course, she has questions when I finally started to act more like myself for the last two weeks.

'Me and some friends. Aditya is going to pick me up.' I had to lie to her. I couldn't tell her that it was a date! I walked past her towards the living room and sat on the sofa with a casual jump beside my dad. My dad was watching the movie *Pilla Zamindar* on ZeeTelugu. My mom followed me and was staring at me with her hands on the hip, blocking the TV. I smiled...

'Amma... What is it? Look, It's just a casual dinner with a friend. He has some coupons for the boat ride, he invited me.' I blurted out.

'Hmmm... First, it was dinner with friends, now it is a casual dinner with a *friend* huh? Okay... Be back by 9:30pm maximum.' She warned.

'Thank you, Maa...!' I said. 'Only because it is Adi. I like that guy.' She said, which brought a smile to my face. My dad interrupted.

'I'm trying to watch something here. What is this drama?'

My mom went back into the kitchen and just then the commercials got done and the movie started. Suddenly an old conversation began to play in my head.

V: Great. Akanksha and I watched Pilla Zamindar.

S: Hey. I watched it with my friends recently. Great movie. Do you like Nani?

V: I loveeeee him. He is my favourite actor.

S: Mine too! I love Surya also.

V: Aw I love Surya too. My other favourite actor! But Nani is my forever!

This movie... the conversation... Subhash... Everything came back to me. I realized my body began to shiver. The sheer pain of it all began to come back. I inhaled sharply and got myself out of the loop. I went into the balcony, holding the parapet real tight, taking deep and desperate breaths of oxygen. I got diverted by the ping of a notification on my phone.

'Hey. I'm here. Do you want me to come up?' Adi texted.

'No. I'll be right there.' I replied and went back inside. I told my dad I was leaving but he was too involved in the movie to even notice me. So, I yelled to my mom saying, 'Maa... Bye. I'm leaving.' And got down the stairs.

'Hey, Adi...! Shall we go?' I said as I was reaching his bike. He nodded and signalled me to hop on. He didn't say much and I was too distracted to say anything either. When we reached, he parked the vehicle on the opposite side of the road to the restaurant. We silently walked acknowledging the awkward air around us. When we reached the edge of the road and hesitated to cross the road, Adi came towards my right side, grabbed my hand and we both crossed the road. He left my hand the second we reached the other side. I looked at him and felt embarrassed. Suddenly it dawned upon me. *Did he even want to come? Is this really what I want?* I was not sure. I saw Aditya talking to the Matre'd and waited in the lounge area. As he was walking towards me, I had visions of how I used to feel about Adi in the first and second years of college. I thought he was very attractive and I always had butterflies in my stomach when he was around. But now, nothing.

'Varna... You said you booked a table, right? He says neither of our names is there...' I frowned and went to the Matre'd and looked at the book.

When I went and checked the book, I saw it... I booked a table under the name Subhash. I was thinking about him and when I called the restaurant I subconsciously said *'A table for Varna and Subhash'*. I froze looking at the names. My legs started to shiver and breathing started to become a little difficult. The Matre saw me changing and kept asking if I was okay. Adi, who was looking at his phone until then, saw me and sprinted towards me. He saw the name and held my arms tight and turned me towards him. He looked me in the eye and said, 'Varna look... Breathe... You are fine. Just breathe okay...'

I nodded and tried but it was of no use. I was losing control. I began to shiver more and I realized I had tears in my eyes. He apologized to the guy and we both came out so that I could get some oxygen. He never let go of me, he held me tight and we both walked a little farther and he sat me down on the footpath once my breathing was controlled.

'Varna... What just happened? Was that the same thing you had back then? A panic attack?' He asked with genuine care and worry for me.

I couldn't answer him right away. I felt very embarrassed so I bent and rested my head on my knees. He put an arm around me and started rubbing my shoulder. That touch felt so platonic. It gave me a sense of comfort and ease to talk to him. I looked up at him and the tear that formed in my eye slowly dropped down my cheek.

'I'm sorry Adi.' I finally said.

'Sorry...? Are you saying sorry because you were about to have a panic attack? Or that you booked a table for us under his name?'

'Both...'

'Varna. You don't have to be sorry for either. I have seen you in love with this guy and I have seen you when he left. But the thing is, are you still in love with him? Does this happen often? I mean mistaking someone else's name to be his?'

'It does Adi. He is my whole world. I love him more than anything and anyone. I still believe he is with me. I see him everywhere. I hear his voice everywhere. Look, that guy... he could be him. He looks like him. See, doesn't he?' I said pointing towards a random guy walking on the other side of the road. Adi looked at him and back at me sympathetically. He just shook his head. I exhaled and continued talking.

'You remember how I fainted and... you know... when he left? It never stopped Adi. It happens all the time. I see someone who looks like him or hear someone that sounds like him on tv or sometimes I dream of him and I run towards my balcony and stare at the silent empty road hoping he is there. And then it starts. The shivering and sweating, I'll lose control of my breathing and this huge fireball inside my heart keeps emerging out to burst out like lava. But then I get myself back to reality. I swallow everything, I close my eyes, take a walk, get some oxygen and I try and divert myself entirely from the scene. I guess that's the reason I have been avoiding anything and everything that reminds me of him, including Akanksha. It was in her room, on her screen that I first saw him, Adi. That smile... it still shines in my heart.' I let out a laugh. The laughter slowly became sad and I could feel the depression creeping through me. He didn't say a word. He just held me and kept rubbing my shoulder.

'Every time I come close to any memory related to him, I begin to panic. I'm hit with the harsh truth that he isn't here anymore. He left Adi...' Tears kept rolling down my calm face. 'I can't show it. It's probably stupid that this still happens, even after an entire year. I can't let my parents know. I can't tell Akanksha. She probably hates the guy more than anyone. But you... Adi, you were the only one I felt comfortable with. You were the one that completely threw me off of his memories. You never try to talk to me about him or you don't care about him which makes it easier for me to forget him when I'm with you. I sit with you, talk to you, listen to your stupid silly jokes and I laugh, I laugh heartfully. But...' I stopped and looked at him.

He suddenly felt so awkward that he took the hand and moved away. He said,

'But? Continue if you are comfortable Varna.'

'Hmmm... You helped me a lot in getting myself together Adi. But I don't love you. I guess I just used you in a desperate attempt to help myself. I'm sorry.'

Strangely, his face began to blossom. His eyebrows and his temples relaxed and his lips turned into a smile. I frowned at this reaction. He looked happy that I said that.

'Ohhh Varna…! You cannot believe how relieved I am to hear you say this. Thank you so much.' He said and gave me a tight side hug which left me in confusion. I looked at him trying to find answers.

'You have given me an insight into how the last year was for you, right? Let me tell you what else was happening around you… I have completely and madly fallen in love with Akshu and I believe she loves me too.'

I widened my eyes and my mouth in shock. Suddenly my heart felt so relaxed and at peace. I let out a happy sigh and I had a thousand questions. 'What…!!!?? Fallen in love? With Akanksha? Oh, and wait you call her Akshu…!!? And SHE LOVES YOU BACK…!!?'

'I mean, I just guess…and hope! Do you remember the first time I came and talked to you guys in the canteen when we had that assignment we had to do together? I went and requested Pramod Sir to have Akanksha in my group. But Akanksha always does her group projects with you, so I had to be stuck with both of you. I was interested in her from the very first day. I was just a little shy and also worried that I might embarrass you! I mean the whole class teased me with you because you had a crush on me. At that point, if I proposed to Akanksha, I don't think even she would have entertained that thought.'

'Yes, she would have kicked your ass if you tried her back then. That's for sure.' I laughed. He was blushing. It was so damn adorable to see this big macho guy turn all curly and tickly on hearing her name.

'Oh that, I'm sure. She loves you more than you know Varna and she protects you in a way that you can't even imagine.' He said with a serious tone and direct eye contact. That made me wonder if he meant more or something else by saying that.

'What do you mean?'

'You have been so stupid to not talk to her about this and went through this shitty year all by yourself. You thought you were going through this alone, therefore, protecting the people you love from being worried about you. But do you know that she has been through a hell of a year alongside you?' That hit me hard. The smiles and the happiness were suddenly consumed by a great deal of guilt and worry.

'What are you talking about Adi?'

'She was constantly worrying about you. She felt so lonely and left out. You were her best friend but you simply built a huge wall and didn't let anyone in. But you know what, she was right there. Right beside that wall, constantly knocking and waiting for you to open up. There were many instances she would be talking to me about you and she would have tears in her eyes. It broke my heart you know.' I covered my face with guilt.

Oh god Akanksha, you sweet bitch! I replayed all the situations she came and sat with me, tried to talk to me about Subhash, she offered to come to my place instead of hers for group studies. I did observe her changing behaviour towards Adi but I just assumed she is becoming close to him because I have been away a lot. It never crossed my mind that she might be interested in him. She never said anything to me. Suddenly anger began to creep up. It was me! It was her best friend. How did she think I'd not be interested to know if she fell in love?

'Varna... It's probably not my place to talk between you guys. I'm sorry.'

'What? No! I had to come here to know what was happening right under my nose. It's okay Adi. But I'm just wondering, why did you come? Why did you agree to this date in the first place?'

'She made me!' He said.

'What...!? Why on earth would she do that?' I let out a burst of concerned laughter.

'She thinks you still have that old crush on me. So, she didn't want to sabotage your mental health again, knowing how 'well' you took your previous break up.'

'She thought I was in love with you and so she sacrificed her love?' I said more to myself than to him. I suddenly stood up and started walking towards our vehicle. Adi stood up too, held my hand and asked me what I was up to.

'Can you please drop me at her place? I need to talk to her. Please?' I was very serious by now. My face gave him major killer vibes probably because he looked scared.

'Varna... Listen. Settle down first. It's too much information dump all of a sudden. Sleep over it. I don't want you to react in a way that you would regret later. And also, to be frank, I'm not sure what you'll say to her if you meet her now and if there is a chance that she might get hurt due to what you said, I'm going to stop you do that at any cost. Whatever she did or said was all because she cares about you like her little sister.'

'Adi... If you think, after knowing what I know now, I would say something to hurt her, you misunderstood our relationship. It's great how you are protecting her and all, but you better know, I love her like my own sister too. So... You chill, okay?' It was more like a sweet warning than just a reassurance.

'Okay... Sorry! But you really can't go.'

'What? Why?'

'Firstly, she told me she would be going out with her family tonight. Secondly, if not in a romantic way, we can still finish this date... as friends maybe?'

I bent my head towards one side looking at him adoringly and thinking to myself how lucky Akanksha got with him and how lucky I am that I'm best friends with him now. We always wanted our partners to be each other's friends too. I let out a deep breath and nodded.

'Yayyyy! Thank God. Let's eat then.' He said dramatically rubbing his hands on his stomach. I laughed and we both proceeded to the nearby street food joint.

We talked about a lot of stuff during dinner. We talked about how me and Akanksha bonded, he told me about their interactions and things like what he likes in her. While I was listening to him talk about Akanksha, I understood how much he loved her and how perfect he was for her. I was also imagining how perfect it would be if we were all together and were good friends. Me, Akanksha, Adi and my Subhash. That night for the first time in almost a year I didn't feel the jitters or I didn't panic when I thought about Subhash. I felt content to see my best friends fall in love. After we finished dinner I promised Adi,

'Let's surprise Akanksha. Her birthday is in a week. We should plan something special for her and maybe you should plan a grand proposal or something. What do you say?'

'Hmmm... I have given myself a deadline to express my love to her, that's until her birthday. So yeah, a birthday surprise by you will throw her off and my proposal will be a surprise. That sounds interesting. Let's plan something.'

The next morning Akanksha was already in class when I came in. She looked at me and back into her book. I smiled to myself imagining what was in store for her in the next few days. I went to her excitedly and sat beside her without saying anything. She looked at me doubtfully and said,

'What is it? You look creepily happy.'

'I sure am' I said teasingly. She was still looking into her book but not reading it anymore. She took a deep breath and brought up the date.

'So, I assume it went well? The date...'

'Oh Yeah. You wouldn't believe it. It was the best. I didn't know that was exactly what I needed for me to get back on track, you know.'

'Yup. Sounds about right. Adi is the best.' She said, still pretending to read. I smiled heartily at that comment, sensing the love she has for him.

Towards the end of the last class, I turned to her and said excitedly, 'I'm coming with you today to your place. And not to study.' She frowned and said, 'Okay... What do you have in mind?' I just winked at her and smiled. She rolled her eyes.

'So, tell me. What is it that you are so excited to share with me? Did something happen last night? Did you kiss or something?' she asked, hiding the pain she was feeling to have to ask that question.

'Didn't Adi tell you? You guys are close friends too, right?' I teased. She looked at me with a doubtful face, sensing something was fishy. But she didn't say anything. She just kept folding the clothes that were thrown on her bed to make room for me to sit.

'He is just a friend.' She answered after a long silence. I was standing right behind her, folding my hands and observing her. She didn't make eye contact with me since the minute I asked Adi out on a date yesterday. I finally decided to break it.

'Akanksha... do you love him?' She suddenly stopped moving. I slowly went around her and sat in front of her on the bed. She was still standing there like a statue and staring into nothingness like she just saw a ghost. I held her arm and pulled her onto the bed to sit beside me. She sat with a thud but didn't say anything.

'Akanksha... I know I have been distant. I'm not justifying but just saying, I have my reasons. But you didn't have to push yourself away from me! You should have talked to me. I'm wondering how many days or nights you must have spent thinking about him or wanting to talk to me about this. Dude, I have been in love too. I know the game; I know the rules...

Anyway, all put aside, I'm here now, aren't I? Look at me. Talk to me.' By this point, I was worried that I have lost her. She didn't respond for a solid minute, then she took a deep breath and said,

'Did he say something to you? Did you guys talk about me? What happened last night Varna?' She wanted answers.

'We talked about me, Akanksha. Me and Subhash, mostly.' That was when she finally made eye contact. Her eyes had a thousand questions. 'And you and him too.' I finally said, definitely noticing a hint of a smile on her face. I continued.

'I don't know what you were thinking, but I don't want Aditya. I love Subhash. With my whole heart. Hell, my everything. I have given my mind, body, heart and my soul to him. I will love him forever. Tell me now, do you love Aditya?' She nodded and blushed which made my heart swell double its size. I smiled and kept looking at her, for her to continue.

'He is the Chandler to my Monica, Varna.' She said, smiling and shrugging.

'Oh my god...!! You found our Prince then. Wow, I'm so happy for you.' I said and hugging her tightly.

'I have been dying to talk to you about it. But I'm not sure if he loves me Varna. The other day I wanted to confess but that got sabotaged because of your date proposal.' She said sarcastically. I laughed and said, 'Chandler loved Monica more than she loved him, Akanksha. Just remember that.'

Chapter - 11

POV- Akanksha

It has been a week since I expressed my feelings towards Adi to Varna. He had been acting differently since their date. He didn't turn up to our regular badminton games and was even avoiding me in college. I didn't understand what to make of it but I was too busy with assignments and my birthday shopping to overthink the situation. So, when he finally came to me asking me if I would be interested to go out with him in the evening on my birthday, I got excited.

My birthday started pretty great. Varna came by my place to wish me early in the morning and we came to college together. As soon as we entered the classroom, Adi bombed confetti near the entrance. Some of my classmates turned towards me and wished me. As I was passing by the board, I saw it was filled with a huge sketch of me in caricature, wishing me Happy Birthday. It was very funny and I laughed heartily. Adi bowed down and took credit for that masterpiece. I loved that goofy side of him. I sat in my place and took a picture of the board before someone erased it. He came and sat beside me and said, 'You like it? It took me an hour to draw that.'

'It is okay...' I said teasingly. He gasped and I laughed and felt an instant relief that he was back to his normal self. Later I asked about the plan he had in mind for the date in the evening. He casually replied, 'What date?' I looked at him, perplexed, which made him burst into laughter. I cursed him under my breath. That evening after the classes, before I could talk to her, Varna left in a hurry. Adi took me to our favourite little ice cream corner near our college.

'By the way, when are you going to wish me, Adi?' I asked.

'What do you mean? I wished... On the board... which you thought was pretty mediocre.'

'That was a gift, I presumed. You didn't wish me.' I said.

'Oh, Little girl... You are 22. That's all you'll get as you keep ageing.'

He gets to my nerves sometimes but there is a level of comfort in that. We ordered our favourite flavour of ice cream, but when it arrived on our table, he didn't even look. He was busy texting someone on the phone. When I kicked his leg from under the table, he looked at me and put the phone aside.

He was busy with the phone again when it was time to leave. I left him to it and went to the counter and paid for the ice cream. When I took the bill and turned back, he didn't even realize I left. I got pissed off and walked right past him saying, 'Have fun with your girlfriend. I'm leaving.'

That was when he finally realized and apologized. Then he said something strange. 'It's not time yet. Let's just go on a ride. What say?'

'What time? Where?' I asked, confused.

'No. I mean... It's your birthday Akshu. You love pani puri right? I'll take you to a great place. Come on.'

'Are you kidding me? We just had ice cream Adi. What's wrong with you?' I said, sounding frustrated and started walking. He suddenly held my hand and when I looked back, he said, 'I just want to spend some more time with you.' I obliged and he took to me on a long bike ride.

After riding for almost thirty minutes, he pulled over and took out his phone. I rolled my eyes and looked away. After sending a text, we resumed our journey and arrived at the house ten minutes later. As I walked towards the gate, he stopped me and gazed into my eyes. My smile faded, and my heart began to race. He got off the bike, slowly walked towards me, leaned over my shoulder, and whispered, "Happy Birthday" in my ear. When he stood back up, he was giggling. I was so mesmerized by him that I was almost ready to kiss him. He then held me by the shoulder, turned me towards the elevator, and said, "Go ahead. They must be waiting for you."

As I ascended in the elevator, I pondered over his words. What did he mean by "they must be waiting?" When I opened the door, I was surprised to see a crowd of people walking around the house, unaware of my arrival. My mom and Varna were busy arranging food and cake on a table in one corner. Some of my classmates and project teammates were there, as well as a couple of my best friends from school who were chatting with my dad and some of our neighbours. Varna noticed me and yelled, "She's here, guys... Surprise...!" Everyone else joined in with her shouting. I thanked everyone and greeted them one by one. I cut the cake, and some of them gave me gifts. The party was a great success, with Varna arranging for us to play Tambola, which most people enjoyed. However, I have never been a fan of the game, so I went up to her and said, "Varna... If you don't mind, please continue the game and engage them. I'll just freshen up and come back."

'Yeah Sure. Go ahead. But before you do, can you do me a small favour? There is some stuff that I left on the terrace. Can you please bring it down for me?'

I was confused initially as to why would she have stuff on my terrace but didn't bother to ask questions. I took the keys to the terrace and climbed the stairs. As I approached the final flight of stairs, I noticed that the terrace door lock was open and the door was banging due to the wind. I frowned thinking who could have gone upstairs when all my friends were down there at my party. When I slowly pushed the door wide open, I was faced with the most beautiful surprise. Adi was standing at the end of a pathway of rose petals with red heart balloons on the sides, wearing a white shirt and blue jeans and holding red roses. It was magical. I put my palms on my cheeks and slowly walked towards him on the rose petals saying, 'Adi... What's going on?'

'Akshu... You are a brilliant and beautiful young woman who stole my heart right from under my nose without any sympathy. I have loved you since the day I laid eyes on you. But knowing me, I needed to be friends first and spend this time with you to realize that you are the one. You are MY one.'

I was so happy and surprised and overwhelmed to stand straight. I was almost about to lose control when he came closer and held me. We locked our eyes and he continued, 'I want to share my life with you. I want to wake up to you, bring coffee to you, work out together and go ahead and conquer the world with you. I want to have ice cream with you and also maybe some kids with you. I want to grow old knowing I'm with you and you are with me.' I laughed but my eyes were a mess. I stood up tall and hugged him tight, messing his brand-new white shirt with my mascara.

Later I took him to the top of the water tank and sat on the edge of it. I rested my head on his shoulder and just savoured that moment. After a little while I said, 'Adi... what you said was beautiful. But how come you never expressed any of these feelings to me, even indirectly?'

'Well, those were not my words. I googled them.' I looked at him with shock and then saw him giggle. I rolled my eyes and pulled his arm into a hug. He looked at me, still laughing. His look communicated more than his goofy smile. He was looking at my lips keenly like he was about to swallow them. At that moment I didn't mind if he wanted to. So, I bent in a little closer and we kissed. I smiled through the kiss and kept kissing until I heard the sound of the terrace door and looked back. It was Varna running away through the terrace door.

POV- Varna

I ran up to the terrace with a lot of curiosity and anticipation. When I opened the terrace door, I didn't find them anywhere around. But I thought the idea was lovely. The rose petals pathway, the balloons. I slowly walked on them, channelling my inner little girl. I looked around searching for them as Aunty was asking where Akanksha was and she wanted her downstairs. There they were on the water tank, kissing. Adi had his arm around her, pulling her closer to him. Her hands were probably on her lap which I couldn't see from behind. The wind was favouring them pushing Akanksha's hair away from her, letting Adi kiss her. I stared at them for several seconds. Suddenly my body was craving Subhash's attention. I subconsciously hugged myself and closed my eyes, trying to feel him. I could see his smiling face, his broad shoulders completely hugging me from behind and I could hear him whisper *I Love you Varna* in my ears with his perfect voice. I shook my head out of the imagination and felt embarrassed that I had those feelings looking at Adi and Akshu kissing. I immediately ran out of the terrace and stood on the stairs trying to pull myself together.

Akanksha probably heard me because she came inside after a few seconds and exclaimed, 'He loves me back Varna...!' and hugged me and we both started jumping. Adi came through the door and cleared his throat.

'Ok now stop hugging my woman. I'm feeling jealous.' He said.

'Oh really? Now that you guys are together, I can't hug my best friend?' I said and hugged her tighter and kissed her on the cheek. She kept looking at him like she was enjoying his jealousy. Adi came forward and pulled her closer to him.

'You can only do that. But I get to do this...' He said and pulled her face and kissed her on the lips which caught me and her off guard. I laughed heartily and said, 'Okay. Enough with your PDA now. People are waiting for you downstairs Akanksha. We need to go.' She wasn't looking at me, but still staring into his eyes. He looked at me and then at her. She held his head and kissed him on the forehead before she left the terrace.

The party was nearing the end. Almost all the neighbours left. Akanksha was still chit-chatting with her school friends. I felt very distracted and disturbed but in a good way. For an entire year, I couldn't even think of Subhash without having to desperately search for oxygen. I have been thinking about him without panicking for a week now since the day I opened up about him to Adi. But today was the first time I was feeling things differently. Not just my soul and my heart but my body wants him. It feels incomplete and empty without him. Suddenly I felt the urge to talk to him again. I went into Akanksha's room and logged into Orkut. It wasn't functioning anymore, with WhatsApp and Facebook being the main platforms of communication. I opened our chat box and started reading all the messages. After about half an hour Akanksha came into the room, exhausted. I immediately closed the chat window and faced her. She fell on the bed with a thud and exhaled.

'The best birthday ever Varna. Thank you so much.'

'Aww... You should be thanking Adi's lips for that. Not me!' We both laughed and she turned towards me, resting her head on her elbow.

'I know you keep saying it was all his plan, but I know you. I can imagine your role in all this. I just want to say Thank you. I loved tonight.' I smiled at her and asked, 'So, how was the proposal by the way? Tell me everything.'

'Ahh... It was beautiful Varna. I was casually walking on the stairs to reach the terrace and the door was banging. When I entered, Adi was standing there with red roses in his hand. All handsome. Hmmm, you should have seen what a beautiful site that was. As I kept wondering and walking towards him, he started talking...' She then told me everything Adi said. She turned all pink and blushed when she was talking about the kiss.

'Haha. Yeah, I caught some of the action too.' I said and we both laughed and she fell back on the bed smiling and staring at the ceiling fan. 'I'm so glad you found your love in Adi. He is the best for you. You complement each other so well.'

'Thank you, Dude. And hey, can you please put this back in my jewellery box over there.' She said and handed me the chain she was wearing. I took the chain and opened her box. While I was putting the chain back, I observed a small hidden rack in her jewellery box from which something was creeping out. I wanted to set it back inside so I opened it and there I saw the letter. The letter Subhash gave me before he left. I grabbed the letter and closed her jewellery box. She looked at me and suddenly sat up straight.

'Varna. I'm sorry. I don't remember that was there. Give it back to me.'

'No. I want to read it.' I said. She looked at me doubtfully with a hint of regret on her face. 'I'm fine Akanksha.'

'Okay... if you say so. I'm going to take a shower. Is that okay?'

'Absolutely. Go ahead.' I sat on the revolving chair and began reading the letter. As I finished reading the letter I stood up, went to the window and started thinking, staring into the beautiful night sky. This time the letter didn't feel as disturbing as it did previously. It was sweet, endearing and wholesome. He had his reasons why he had to leave without meeting me. He was decent enough to at least give it closure, even if it was through a letter. He genuinely sounded apologetic and sad for doing that. And then it hit me. He mentioned that he loves me at the end. What if he didn't want to leave me? What if it was more of a cry for help? What if he genuinely wanted to be together but wondered if I would be okay with it? I ran back to the desk and read the letter again...

So, I guess I'm trying to say... this is it for us. I cannot keep in contact with you while I'm there. And I cannot ask you to wait around for me for another 2-3 years without really knowing what is going to happen. That's not fair. And you are a great catch Varna. Anyone would be lucky to have you. I can't ask you to hold on for me when I'm not sure when I'd return and when I'd start my career. It's just too much to ask.

I would like to say one last thing. I LOVE YOU Varna. With my heart, body, soul and all that I am. I love you now, I loved you for all those years I didn't have you by my side and I loved you even when we were little kids. Even when I didn't know what love meant. And I will love you for as long as I breathe. You were my angel. You are my angel... You are my own personal fairy angel who came into my life to show me the purpose of life.

What was he thinking? Why didn't he talk to me about this, with all the shit we used to talk about every day? What did he mean by '*I can't ask you to hold on for me... It's just too much to ask.*'

Of course, he can! And even if he didn't, I would wait for him. I love him. He didn't even give me a chance to tell him that. Or was that on purpose? He sure knew I was in love with him. He said '*he would love me for as long as he breathes.*' If he was so sure about his love, why didn't he feel confident about it and tell me or ask me to wait for him? Instead, he gave an ultimatum saying this is it for us.

Everything started to seem different. I became restless and started pacing the room, reading the letter again and again, wanting answers. Just then Akanksha came into the room, saw me like that and panicked.

'Varna... Are you okay? You look weird. Please talk to me.'

'He was trying to tell me something. I didn't get it back then but I guess I do now. He wanted more. He probably needed me to read between the lines.'

'What are you talking about? Yes, he did want to tell you something. That he was an asshole and that he was leaving you.'

I suddenly stopped moving and gave a death glare at her and started packing my things to leave.

'Varna... I'm sorry. But be practical. He mentioned everything clearly. He couldn't even do that to you on your face. I don't want you to start building something again where there is nothing. I mean he didn't even try to make contact with you for a year. He probably forgot the entire thing. Please understand.' I took my bag and just left without responding to her.

I went straight into my room without greeting my mom or dad who were sitting in the living room and threw my bag on the floor. I left everything there and went inside to take a shower. Water calms me down, so I just stood there under the running water and closed my eyes trying to figure out what this mess was. I have a thousand questions. Suddenly, Subhash doesn't feel like something that happened to me a few months ago. He has always been there. I still feel him, see him, hear him like he is right beside me. And now the letter just opened up so many loose ends. I need to tie them all up for my peace of mind. *What happened to him from the time he texted me for the first time to the time he left me that letter? What changed? Why did he feel the need to write a letter rather than meet me? Why mention that he loves me at all when he was planning to leave? It was not like we were ever in a relationship, we never committed to each other, never made any promises and never called ourselves boyfriend/girlfriend. Then why? Why did he have to mention that just before he left? Is there something bigger? Is there something that I'm not able to see?*

I came out of the shower with a determination to do something about it. Subhash is someone I feel very passionate about. I can't let him go just like that. That's not me. I like something, I always go after it until I get it or until I convince myself that I'm not made for it. I guess that's exactly what I need right now. I need to figure him out and understand if this is the ultimate thing to do or if there is something that could be done to make this happen and work. That night after dinner I went on to the terrace and sat on the grill staircase. My dad walked towards me, sat beside me and said,

'Do you know what is Petrichor?' I was completely taken aback by this random thing he was asking.

'A What?'

'Petrichor is that unique earthy smell you feel before it rains.'

I frowned at him still not understanding why he was telling me that. He looked at me and then finally asked, 'What is bothering you Varna?'

Then it hit me that it was his way of diverting me from my stress and calming me down. I smiled at how adorable he was and how well that works on me. I rolled my eyes, put my head on his shoulder and said, 'Subhash...'

He didn't respond for an entire minute and I was too distracted to see what his reaction was. Then he asked, 'I thought you moved on...'

'Moved on? Never Nanna. I guess I only love him more than ever if that's even possible. I never moved on and I never will.'

'Okay, I can't pretend like that doesn't bother me Kanna. Didn't he leave, throwing a letter at you?'

'Exactly. He did it with a letter. That's not like him. He loved me, Nanna. I felt it. Maybe it is possible to lie about a few things but It's not possible to fake a connection... I think there is more to it. I need to find out.'

'What do you mean? Do you want to contact him?'

'No. I don't think so, although that's something I would love to do. I'm craving his love Nanna but this is different. I need to understand what he had gone through.'

'Okay... Still not able to get you. What is it that you want to do?'

'I should probably go to Vizag.'

'What...!? Are you kidding me?'

'No Nanna, think about it. That makes perfect sense. I need to know. I must go.'

He didn't respond, but it was clear that he was not comfortable with this proposal. He was thinking, probably how to say no to me. But then I interrupted his thought process.

'I'll take Akanksha with me. And Adi too! I'll have company. If nothing turns up it'll just be like a small trip with friends. How about that?'

'Hmmm... That sounds okay. Wait, Isn't Aditya that guy you went on a date with the other day?'

'Oh yeah, that's him. Akanksha and him are a couple now by the way.' I said and stood up in a hurry to run to my mom and tell her that I'm going on a trip with my friends. It took a little while for my dad to process that and when he did, he stood up and came running behind me asking about Adi and Akanksha, a little shocked.

That night I had the most special dream ever. It felt like validating what I was feeling and assuring me that it was the right step to take at this point.

Subhash was walking on one side of the street, holding a coffee cup in one hand and holding the phone to his ear with the other. He was wearing a black turtle neck shirt, grey trousers, a brown jacket, brown shoes and black sunglasses. I was standing on the other side of the street just looking at him and admiring him and his style. He looked like a male supermodel walking on the ramp. He was extremely stylish, just as I remember him from my childhood. In a place full of oversized t-shirts and baggy pants, Subhash looked like a diamond in his formals. He turned to cross the road but his demeanour changed when he noticed me there. He left the cup he was holding, spilling coffee all over the footpath. He cut the call and put the phone into his jacket and without even looking at the road he just started walking towards me. I was looking at him doubtfully, regretting my decision to just show up. But he came to me and hugged me tightly, not giving my body any space to even breathe. The hug was not romantic but emotional. The very handsome, strong, rock-solid man that I just saw suddenly became this vulnerable, soft person. Probably he felt the hug wasn't enough, he lifted me and rotated me, holding me tighter every second. The minute he put me down I saw his eyes swelled up. I was shocked to see him like that. When I asked him why, he said, 'Finally, I found you. I have been so lost, losing you. Now, just knowing that you're back, I can die peacefully.'

I said, 'Well, I didn't come all the way here just to see you die, Mister!' He laughed heartily, grabbed my face in his hands and kissed me. Right there in the middle of the University of

Pennsylvania. We kissed for several minutes and he lifted me into the air again and I laughed.

The next morning, Akanksha was waiting for me at the parking lot, worried. The minute I entered the gate I could see relief in her eyes. She stood beside me while I parked and said,

'Dude, I'm so sorry. How are you? I spoke to Adi yesterday. He told me about your panic attacks shit. Are you kidding me with that? That doesn't sound normal or healthy. Why the hell didn't you tell me?'

'Whoa...Calm down. I'm completely fine now.' I said while removing my helmet.

'What do you mean calm down? Does your dad know? He had been calling me now and then, the whole of last year, trying to find out what was going on with you. And I feel stupid that neither of us knew you were going through this. That's not fair you know.' We started walking towards the classes by now.

'Akanksha. Listen, I need you to calm down. Because I have something to tell you.'

'No. I'm pretty mad at you right now. And what do you want to tell me?'

I smiled excitedly, grabbed her arm and pulled her towards the canteen.

'What? The class begins in 3mins.'

'This is more important. Come on,' I said. We went into the canteen; I sat her down at our spot and got coffees for the both of us.

'Okay. Tell me.'

'I decided... that...'

'Yes?'

'...to... pursue Subhash harder.' She choked on her coffee.

'Are you fucking kidding me right now, Varna?'

'He is THE one for me. I believe it with all my heart, now more than ever. I love him, Akanksha, with everything I have got. So, I'm going to try with everything I have got, to get him back.' She held her head with both her hands and shook her head.

'Akanksha. The universe wants us back. It's been hinting at me all this while and I ignored it until yesterday. But now I know. This is it.'

'What do you mean?' She asked, looking exhausted.

'So, you now know about the attacks, right? They happened every single time I thought to myself that this is over. And I had to go out, breathe and shake that thought off to get better. Do you know when it stopped? After an entire year, when I finally embraced the fact that he is the one for me. When I told myself that this is not the end and I'm not going to give up on him. I'm able to think of him, talk about him, say his name out loud without any hint of that shit happening again.'

'Oh, God... Varna. Isn't it a possibility that "time" happened? With passing time and distance, you probably moved on or maybe he doesn't mean as much to you as before but you are not able to admit it to yourself?'

'No. I don't think he means any less to me, Akanksha. I love him more than ever! Okay, if you don't want to go with the Universe theory, I have something else for you... Do you remember after the day the first panic attack happened? You asked me what I think about the whole thing. I didn't know back then. I didn't want it to end and so I didn't want to act on it. That day, I told you that I will tell you or I will take a decision about what to do with the letter when I have clarity on the matter. And after all this while, I feel in my gut that this is what I have to do.'

She processed what I said for a while and slowly said, 'Okay... if you say so. I'm your friend and please remember that I'm here, whatever it is that you're going through, okay? No more hiding panic attacks and shit, got it?'

'I'm not going to get them anymore. What did I just explain to you?' She rolled her eyes and asked, 'So, what's your plan?'

'I want to go to Vizag.'

'What for? He isn't there right?'

'No. But he was. He was there when he first met me. And he was there when he decided to leave me. We talked about having a relationship in the beginning if you remember. I need to know what happened in between. What made him change? What made him go from wanting me to leaving me. And I believe he didn't want to leave me. Look at the letter. It sounds to me like he secretly still wanted me, but was not sure if I would wait for him. Here, read it.' I handed the letter to her. She looked at me doubtfully and read the letter again. After she finished reading it, she inhaled sharply and said, 'Okay... you can go but with one condition. I'm going with you.' I smiled and hugged her.

'I know you would say that. That's why I already told my parents that I'm going with you and Aditya. You guys can have a little romantic trip while I explore my boyfriend.' She laughed, looking excited.

'I would love that but I need to ask Adi though.'

Chapter-12

'Nanna... Maa already packed food for all of us to eat. I don't need all these...' I told my dad who brought us chips packets and 1ltr bottle of *Maaza* from the small kiosk on the Secunderabad Railway station platform.

'Yeah, of course, that's what you are going to eat. These are just for munching before dinner. It's a long journey. Anyway, where is this boy? It's getting late!' He kept looking at the stairs coming onto the platform, waiting for Adi.

'He is on his way Uncle. He'll be here in 5 minutes. Don't worry.' Replied Akanksha, understanding my dad's anxiety.

'Okay... It's just... The train will start in 8 minutes and you didn't even board yet.'

'Uncle... The bags are already inside. You and Varna can go sit inside if that's okay. I'll meet Adi and get him in.' My dad jumped on the offer before I could say anything and pulled me into the train. We went to our seats and he sat in front of me.

'Kanna, I know I agreed to your stupid plan but I'm worried for you. What if you find out something you don't want to hear? I don't know what you are expecting out of this but it all seems like a very far shot.'

'If not anything I'll just roam around, see the campus, enjoy the beach and come back. I'm not expecting anything at all. I don't know what it is that I'll find out but my gut says it's the right thing to do. You have trusted me in many situations where you shouldn't even be. This is my life, Nanna, my future I'm talking about here. I believe in it. I want you to trust me again. Please...' His face still showed a lot of valid anxiety but he nodded and kissed me on the forehead.

'I do trust you Kanna. Or else I wouldn't have agreed to this whole thing at all. I'm just worried about you getting hurt again.' He expressed. I reassured him by holding his hand. Meanwhile, Akanksha and Adi came to the seat and Adi greeted my dad. They both shook hands and my dad left.

During the entire journey to Vizag, I saw a completely different side of Akanksha. I haven't imagined her as anything else other than a great best friend. But seeing her as Adi's girlfriend is fascinating. She has a different glow to her face, a different shine to her smile. Adi brings that out of her and it's too adorable to not notice. I just felt stupid to not see this developing right in front of my eyes. We all had the *rotis* and *aloo curry* that my mom packed for the three of us, discussing Telugu movie releases and our favourite heroes. Adi and Akanksha sat near the window holding hands and whispering into each other's ears and laughing, their whispers covered by the loud noise of the train moving in the night. I went on to the top berth and retired early wanting the night to pass on quickly so that I can step into Subhash's world.

It was a pleasant winter morning, slightly sunny with a hint of cool breeze. I was sitting on a beach mat taking out food that I packed from the picnic basket and setting it in use-and-throw plates. I looked at Subhash playing with our 3year old twin boys in the water and smiled to myself, rubbing my 7-month pregnant belly. He lifted both the kids on each of his biceps and rotated them around. 'Careful...!' I yelled at them. He dropped them but they kept asking him, 'Once more Nanna please.' He looked at me smiling and shrugging and did it again. I finished setting the food on the plates and called them out. Subhash came first and sat beside me kissing me on the cheek first and then on my belly. The boys repeated the same and began hogging over their plates. Before beginning to eat, Subhash bent over, kissed my neck romantically and whispered into my ear, 'I hope this one's a girl.' I laughed, looked him in his eyes, kissed his beautiful lips gently and said, 'I do, too.'

The next morning was mostly a blur as I was still pondering the dream. We got off the train and went to the room we booked near Rishi Konda, near the GITAM University campus. We freshened up and went to GITAM, only to know that we would be allowed inside only if we had someone on the inside. It was very devastating at first but Aditya caught hold of a first-year student from the Mechanical department who was entering the college and bribed him to take us in. As we walked on the main road of the campus my heart was pounding. Just the thought that Subhash was here for four years, walking on the same roads, breathing the same air felt very special. We went straight to the engineering block. Adi stopped a girl in the corridor and asked about Subhash. She said, 'Why do you want to know about him?'

'Just like that. We are old friends of his, so....' said Aditya, not finding a better explanation. She looked at us doubtfully for a minute and finally said, 'One of his batchmates is working as assisting faculty here. Maybe he can help you. Go and meet Mr Sandeep in the staff room. I believe he is free now.' We all jumped in excitement and high-fived each other. Before we could thank the girl, she left. We went to the staff room and asked for Mr Sandeep.

'Yes? I'm Sandeep. What is it?' He asked.

'Bro. Can we talk to you outside for a bit?' Aditya asked. He looked at us and asked, 'You are not students, right?' We all looked at each other but before we could answer he got up from his chair and came out of the room. I was too excited to not say anything until we settled. I asked immediately, 'Did you study with Subhash?'

'Yes... He was my batchmate. Why? What about him?'

'We wanted to ask a few questions about him, bro. If you don't mind, can we sit somewhere other than here?'

'Sure. But I don't know what you'll get out of me! I knew him as a hostel mate more than a classmate. We are both from different branches, so...'

'Did you play cricket with him? Thursday nights? Or maybe have you ever been to one of those secret terrace parties that you guys used to have in the hostel?' I asked, with no chill whatsoever.

'Hmmm... Yeah, sometimes we played together. He was good!' I smiled proudly. 'But he stopped playing in the last semester. He used to be seen a lot less too. Like maybe once in two weeks or so. I have heard my friends talk about how much he has changed and was not available in college and all.'

'Was he missing classes?'

'Initially, a lot. But in the final year, he became more serious. His grades improved a lot. He was seen around the staff room very often asking doubts and some extra lessons, I think. Yeah, he went mad during the final semester.'

'Do you know why?' I curiously asked.

'Hmmm, as I said, we were not close. I'm sorry. Oh yeah, he used to go out a lot, with that senior guy... I don't remember his name. Maybe he would know something.'

'Gowtham...!?' I asked, in surprise and relief that I found someone who can give me more answers.

'Yes...! They spent a lot of time together. Gowtham used to come and pick Subhash all the time.' He said.

'Okay. Thank you so much.' I said and shook his hand.

'So what is this about? Is something wrong?' He asked with curiosity.

'No bro. All is well. Thank you.' Aditya replied and pushed us to move so we don't have to answer more questions.

We went to the *Vennela* canteen on campus to grab some coffee. Aditya pulled a chair for Akanksha and signalled that he'd get us coffee. I was too occupied with my thoughts to say anything but Akanksha wouldn't leave me alone.

'So? What do you think? The whole seriousness and improving grades and all? Did you guys ever talk about stuff like that?'

'Yeah, we did. He used to tell me if he had assignments and he used to feel very torn that he had to stop talking to me to go to study. I used to say I admire that he is giving more importance to studies than before.'

'Hmmm. You told me he wasn't like this when you started talking right? There must have been some influence from you, Varna. Your aura rubs off on people you know. That's why I like you.' I looked at her and smiled, my mind still not completely present. I inhaled deeply and looked out the window recollecting a conversation we had.

'I guess my friends are all a little pissed with me that I'm not spending as much time as I used to previously.' He said.

'Ohh... Maybe you should then. I need to study anyway.'

'Hmmm. But I love talking to you Varna. It gives me the energy to get through tomorrow. I'm nervous about this presentation.'

'Nah. Come on. I think it looks great. Just believe in yourself, go on that stage and block everyone out. You'll do good. Trust me.'

'Haha. If I block everyone out, I'll see you sitting in front of me and smiling.'

'So? Do that... It'll be just like how you explained everything to me now. I'll cheer you on and listen to your presentation. Forget there are other people. You'll be fine. Come on now... go through the presentation and the notes once again and go spend some time with them. All the best for tomorrow.'

We had coffee and chatted for a little bit and then Aditya asked, 'So, what now?'

'We go to Gajuwaka. He used to work with this friend who owned a fusion food joint. Maybe he can tell us something. He spent most of his time there.'

'Okay... Do you know the name of this joint?' Akanksha asked.

'No... But I know who owns it. Gowtham.' I said.

'Okay... Now we just have to hit all the food joints and ask if it's owned by a Gowtham. Oh boy, this could take a while then.' Adi commented and I laughed.

We went to Gajuwaka and searched for food joints. There were around 30 of them. We narrowed it down to fusion food and we got around 7, so we started visiting them. By the time we visited five, it was almost 3 pm and we were pretty tired. Aditya suggested we could go back to the room, rest for a bit and come back later. I was ready to keep going for another few hours though. I was so optimistic because everything seems to be pointing at this one guy. I requested them to hold on and told them I would speed up the process. When we finally entered the sixth food joint and settled on a table. I went to the counter and looked for someone to talk to. I found a guy cleaning the waffle iron in one corner and asked him about the owner and his name. He said that he was new and he didn't know much around here and his boss just went for lunch. He also mentioned that it would be evening by the time his boss would be back.

We decide to take a break and went back to the hotel. Akanksha and Aditya slept as soon as they reached. I was feeling restless. I paced around the room, anticipating what could happen when I meet Gowtham. I know it's not exactly meeting Subhash but I feel I'm close to knowing him and his truth and his side of the story. That gave me goosebumps. I saw a notepad and a pen on the side table and grabbed it and started writing.

Subhash... First things first. I love you so very much.

I came to Vizag in search of more information about you and to know where you came from when you decided to leave abruptly. But now that I'm here I don't think I care. I don't need to know that. I'm loving this experience of being in the same places as you were and connecting the places to memories that you shared with me. It all feels real. I'm yet to meet Gowtham and the anticipation is killing me. I'm looking at the ocean from my window and I feel I'm ready. I'm all in Subhash. I could cross this ocean for you. To meet you. To be with you. The distance between us has only made my love towards you that much stronger. I don't think I can ever settle down until I reach you...

Yours Forever, Varna.

I shut the notepad and stood beside the window staring into the ocean. The vision of him, me and our children, the dream kept coming back to me. I was looking at the beach and smiling to myself when Adi came and stood beside me. He stretched and leaned over the window facing me.

'What is it Varna? Are you okay?' He asked.

'Yeah absolutely. More than okay Adi. I don't know what I'll find out but just being here makes me happy. Yesterday when we started, I felt a little stupid to travel 700kms, not knowing what to expect, not knowing whom to meet, what to ask...'

'Yeah. We couldn't say it to your face but we did think this whole idea was stupid.' He said casually to which I laughed.

Just then Akanksha woke up and said,

'Ok, Varna. Shall we begin round two?' I turned my face and said,

'I thought you said this idea was stupid.' I asked teasingly.

'Of course, it is. But I'm all in. If this is what you want, then this is what we'll do.' She said walking towards us.

'Thank you so much guys for coming along.' I said, sounding emotional. Adi came closer and hugged both of us. We dispersed from our group hug and started getting ready to check out the rest of the two food joints on our list.

The little bell on the top of the door alerted the guy at the counter of our arrival. He wasn't the same person we met before. He turned around looked at me and stopped moving. He kept staring at me like he saw a ghost. He was a lean, tall guy with a top knot and mild beard. It looked like he was hitting on me as he was smiling at me creepily. As we were all hungry, we decided to grab some food first so Akanksha went to order food at the counter. The whole while she was ordering food, he kept throwing glances and smiles. He took the order and gave it to another guy working behind him. He came around the counter and walked straight to us.

'Hello, madam. How are you doing today?' He asked, looking directly at me.

'Very well. Thank you.' I said, smiling at him. He still kept staring at me which made me feel awkward. Aditya observed that and said,

'We are well too brother. Now can we get our order please?'

'Of course, Sir. But if you agree, I would like to give your order as a complimentary mam.' He said looking at me.

'Why?' asked Akanksha folding her hands and leaning back into the chair. He looked at Akanksha and turned to me again and said,

'Well. You are beautiful mam and your presence uplifted the aura of this place.'

'Whoa... You're hitting on her? That's bold!' Akanksha said teasingly.

'I'd like to believe when you find something worthy, try with everything you have to get it.' He said smiling at Akanksha. We were all taken aback by his forwardness. 'Oh God...!' Akanksha exclaimed, laughing.

'What is it that you want, mister?' I asked.

'Mam. Firstly, I'd like to know your name. Secondly, would you like to go out on a date with me? I'll make it worth your while.' Adi and Akanksha seemed to be pleasantly shocked and they looked at me trying to hide their smiles.

'Okay look... You are coming on a little strong. I have a boyfriend. But I can give you this... my name is Varna.' The second he heard my name he gasped. His smile vanished and his face turned into a big question mark with shock. We began to wonder what was wrong, but before we could ask him anything he said, '...Are you Subhash's Varna?'

I sat up straight and asked, 'Gowtham? Is that you?'

'Yes! Yes, sister. That's me. Oh my god... Subhash told me a LOT about you but never mentioned you were THIS beautiful...!' He said dramatically pointing both his hands at me. I was so overwhelmed to have finally found him that I completely ignored his comment.

'Gowtham. We came here to meet you.'

'Meet me? Why? And suddenly I'm feeling embarrassed that I hit on you. You are like my sister!' I held both his arms and said,

'Water under the bridge, it is okay. We came to Vizag to find out what happened with Subhash. Can you help us?' I was desperate to hear what he had to say. Meanwhile, our order came in. Gowtham took the order from the waiter guy and placed it on our table and asked him to turn the *Closed* sign on the door and pull the blinders. He asked the guy to take the shift off and leave. Once he left, Gowtham sat with us at our table and began talking.

'Varna... What do you mean by what happened with Subhash? I only know till the part where he bid me goodbye to leave for the US and told me he would meet you in Hyderabad before he leaves. Didn't he?'

'He never made it to Hyderabad.' Akanksha said with a hint of anger in her voice.

'He sure did. I was there when he boarded the bus to Hyderabad. He said he would meet his friend Madhu there.'

'I met Madhu. He was the one who gave me the gift.'

'The chocolate gift? Yeah, I remember the effort he put into getting you all of those. We shopped together. But why would he not give them himself? He was so excited to meet you when he left.' Akanksha and me looked at each other and she rolled her eyes.

'He never met me, Gowtham. It was Madhu who gave me the gift. And he also gave me the letter Subhash wrote.' I said, to which he looked at me, clueless. I opened my bag and handed the letter to Gowtham. He looked at us doubtfully and opened the letter to read it. As he finished reading, he fell back roughly onto the chair and started rubbing his fingers on his forehead. 'Oh Subhash...!' he muttered to himself.

'What is it? Tell me... I came all the way here to know what happened. He was interested to start a relationship in the beginning. What changed?' He looked at me for a few seconds thinking about where to start maybe. And he finally started shaking his head and said, 'He changed. Everything about him changed. Because of you.'

'What do you mean because of me?'

'He loves you but you were more like his *guru* than a friend or a girlfriend... He was just a silly teenager playing around when he joined college. I still remember the first day I saw Subhash. He was chatting and laughing with a bunch of his friends in the canteen during class hours. I wondered what he was doing missing classes. I saw him pretty often. He was seen everywhere around the campus. He was very charismatic. He used to talk to senior girls a lot. Especially Mahima and her gang. I believe she had taken a special interest in him which got him into trouble with senior boys.

Then he started playing cricket with the boys. Things changed after that. The seniors took him in. He was very good at getting things done so they always wanted him around. Not just for the matches but also in general. He was seen with every gang that ever existed in almost three different batches. He was very popular. He had a lot of help to study and get through exams. He never failed even one subject, although I always wondered how considering he always put studies as the last priority. This was how he was for the first two years.

In my final year one day, I was sitting in the canteen, figuring out the detailed plan to get this food joint executed. I was alone juggling with a bunch of papers flying around due to the wind. He came into the canteen and helped me pick them up from the floor. He had this assuring smile, you know. Like telling me it's all going to be okay. I felt calm. He was about to leave when I stopped him and asked if he was free. I needed help with the drawings. He hesitated for a second but later helped me. He asked me about the food joint, why am I doing it and what does it take and all. He was curious and a great foodie himself, just like me. So, after we finished discussing this, I offered to take him out to this hidden gem of a place near MVP colony, to show him what I was looking for in my joint. He probably freaked out you know, a guy asking a guy out. He got all awkward and uncomfortable. I told him that it was okay if he didn't want to. He said he was sorry and ran away. It was funny.' He laughed a bit talking about how he met Subhash. I felt a certain kind of peace listening to him talk about Subhash.

'What happened later? How did you guys meet again?'

'I guess almost two months later. I had already opened the joint by then, to which I invited him but he didn't turn up. He was sitting alone in the canteen one day, staring out the window, looking pretty intense. I went up to the counter, took my food, came back and sat in front of him... no response. Then I initiated the conversation. *Sorry Anna. Tell me. I didn't see you come.* He said, still thinking deeply and very distracted. I asked him what happened. He looked at me, maybe thinking if he can talk to me about it, and he finally said, 'I guess life... happened.' He said, which I didn't understand. He shook his head off and asked quite a lot of questions about my food joint. That is when he told me he was interested in the food business and asked if he can come to the store once to check it out. I agreed and he came.'

I looked around the place and thought to myself, Subhash was here. I felt his presence again. I hugged myself and rubbed my arms imagining he was with me, holding me.

'He was very involved in the process you know. I was surprised by how much interest he took in this place. His change was evident. He stopped hanging out a lot. He went to classes and also joined a study group I believe. As soon as he finished his study commitments he would come running to the store and invest himself here. I imagined he was interested to earn some money but he refused to get paid. He said something like *'The biggest lessons you learn from life come from the most unexpected people and you can never repay them for what they are for you and money can definitely not do that and to me, you are one such friend Anna. So please let me just hang around. I don't want money."*

Aditya interrupted him and asked, 'So what do you think made him change? I still don't see where Varna fits in this equation.'

'Obviously, I got curious one day and asked him. That's when he talked about you for the first time. And believe me when I say this, when he talked about you, I had goosebumps listening to him.'

'What did he say?' I asked, blushing.

'Let me phrase that conversation for you.

Subhash: Varna... That's her name. Do you know what that means?

Gowtham: Ooh lovely. Girlfriend story? Who is she? Your class? Do I know her?

Subhash: My childhood sweetheart. She was my everything. I always looked up to her, loved her, cared for her. But Bangalore happened and I was too excited that I ignored her completely.

Gowtham: Okay?...

Subhash: But recently I met her on Orkut and we started talking. It's unbelievable, the woman she has become...

A wise soul... That's what it means...her name. It also means Goddess Saraswati, which she totally is.

Gowtham: Okay... Tell me more. You are falling for her huh?

Subhash: Completely. I'm madly in love with her.

Gowtham: Oh wow. Did you tell her that then?

Subhash: That's what it is. I don't think I ever can.

Gowtham: What do you mean? You said you love her. Does she have a boyfriend?

Subhash: No. She deserves someone better...

'Whoa. That's crazy. Then what happened?' Adi asked, curiously. All this anticipation and finally when I'm hearing about him and his words about me, I had a lump forming in my throat.

'He began to take life seriously and work towards his passion when he met you. He struggled for a bit but he realized his passion towards business and one day he told me he was preparing for GRE to pursue MBA and then he would come back and open up a restaurant chain. It was all you Varna. That was very clear to me. It changed his entire course of life. He tried every day to do better. He said he needed to make himself worthy of your love. I even asked at one point if you were putting all this pressure on him and forcing him to change.' He pointed at me. I frowned and shook my head.

'Yeah. I know you didn't. Because you never got to the part where you confessed your love to each other. Who are you people...!? I don't get it. It was clear that you loved him too. You spoke to each other a lot. Didn't you?'

'Yes. We had a lot of fun. We discussed movies, hobbies and general world affairs. We would pick up any random topic and share our views. It was very easy with him. I felt comfortable and at home. I used to tell him a lot about how I wanted my life to be. I talked about my career plans, my goals and stuff like that.'

'That's very romantic.' He said sarcastically and rolled his eyes. 'You should have told him at least. Why didn't you say anything?'

'I wanted to. I was desperate to. But I was hoping to do that when we met. So, I waited.'

'Yeah. And he kept developing his love for you by the second. You know sometimes it felt too overwhelming, even to me, to see him like that. He loved you with every ounce of his body. He took so much from you. He looked up to you. Learnt what is love and what is joy. He said suddenly everything became clear to him and he realised what life is and that it was you...' I smiled with my heart knowing that he found himself and truly felt connected with his soul.

'Varna. I don't think I have ever seen love like that. Subhash loved you with his whole heart and soul. He believed you were soulmates. You know that woman,

Mahima... she was hitting on him. She made many passes too. She was desperate to have him but he didn't budge at all. Once I asked him to show me a picture of you. He said he didn't have one. I was so shocked. I insisted so he showed me a picture he had from your childhood.'

'Which picture was it?'

'The one where you were both sitting on the stairs and talking to each other. He mentioned that his dad took that picture without both of you knowing.' The lump in my throat became bigger and began to push tears out of my eyes. I covered my mouth controlling them, not understanding what they meant. Akanksha stood up, came behind my chair and hugged me from behind.

'So, you are saying, he loved her a lot. But didn't believe he was worthy enough of her, so he left?' Aditya asked trying to connect everything.

'I guess... Or maybe he decided to prove himself to be worthy of her. I mean the whole GRE episode started that way.'

'What happened on the night before he started to Hyderabad? I remember he was off. He kind of snapped at me too.'

'Snapped at you...!? Whoa. Yeah, I mean I remember him being moody and lost in thought. He told me he was going to Hyderabad to meet you and then from there to Bangalore. He also mentioned that it would be unfair to ask you to wait around for him. He was torn to decide. And he decided to break it off instead of making things more complicated.'

'Why would it be complicated? We would have done long distance…! Communication is a lot easier now with WhatsApp, isn't it?'

'Yeah… But…' He hesitated to continue. I understood and nodded. There was silence in the room for the next five minutes.

'How amazing is it that you came all the way here to find out about him!? Seems like you still love him…?'

I inhaled deeply and said, 'More than he could ever imagine.' *Stupid guy,* I muttered under my breath and continued, 'You mentioned this girl Mahima? What about her?'

'Oh, she was his senior, our batch-mate. She fell for him the first day she laid eyes on him. She used to rag him a lot and then ask him to drop her at the hostel. She kept him around her all the time. I believe she was friends with him even though he rejected her multiple times. She must know more about you and his change. Because she was one person he never let go of.'

'He never mentioned her to me…' I said, thinking.

'Well… You are here anyway. I don't think it'll hurt to meet her right?'

I was surprised. 'She is here?'

'Yes... She works at an engineering firm two buildings away. I see her all the time.'

'Can we meet her?' Akanksha asked before I could.

'I guess... She leaves for her home in about 10 mins.'

'Thank you so much Gowtham and Sorry for troubling you.'

'No! I always believed in Varna and Subhash's story and it's my pleasure to be a part of it.'

Later we met Mahima and introduced ourselves. At first, she was annoyed with me but then Akanksha convinced her to talk. We went to the beach and sat on the sand and she slowly started opening up.

'I loved him... I still do! I don't know what you want from me.'

'Mahima... Varna loves him too. She came to Vizag to see if she can make things work between them. She needs this. Please help us.' Akanksha tried to persuade her. She sat quietly for a while and then started talking. I noticed her eyes tearing up.

'I tried to hide my love for him for a year at the beginning. But later I expressed my love shamelessly many times and he kept rejecting me. I was in a constant struggle of love and anger with him. He always treated me like a friend. And then you happened... I had to see the love of my life, fall for someone and go crazy for them, right in front of my eyes. Do you know how torturous that was? It killed me.'

I placed my hand on her shoulder gently and said, 'I'm sorry Mahima. He probably didn't mean to.'

'Oh, please stop talking to me like you know him. Okay? He was with me. I saw him day in and day out. I saw his struggle and his growth.'

I understood her pain and remained silent for the rest of the conversation.

'I saw him being hard on himself to make you believe he was good enough for you. Hell… he was enough for me just the way he was but he didn't care about my feelings. He changed but he changed for good. But I felt the pain watching that caterpillar turn into a butterfly.'

She was staring into the ocean with tears flowing down her cheeks. I couldn't help but sympathize with her. Nobody spoke for the next 10 minutes. She slowly got herself together and said, 'I'm sorry Varna… To blame you for my pain. I guess I just envy you…'

'It's okay Mahima. I understand. We both love him immensely. Let's just celebrate him today, okay?'

'Oh god, Varna… You are a gem of a person. He was right about you. But you need to know something too. Subhash is no less… He is very kind and considerate. He always took care of me. Even though he never reciprocated my love, he made sure I don't take it out on myself because for a while there I was almost about to get addicted to drinking. He pulled me out of it and stayed with me. He held my hand and helped me be a better person till the last second. And the irony was when I thanked him, he said the credit was yours. He said he had learnt to be a good friend and a good person from you. So, I guess... I have to thank you in some way.'

I smiled proudly for the person Subhash was for her.

'Varna... If you do get him, don't ever leave him. He is a boon.'

I nodded and said, 'Never...'

That night while we were heading back to Hyderabad, Akanksha asked me, 'So? What are you thinking Varna? Did anything change for you?'

'Hmmm... I don't know. If it did its only for the better. I love him more than ever. That's the truth and the bottom line. But I'm kind of angry. He should have trusted me to wait for him. Right?'

'Look. Till today I had the least opinion of him in my head. But after what I heard from Gowtham and a lot that I heard from Mahima, I realize he is a great guy and I kind of understand what Subhash must have gone through.'

'You do?' I asked, curious to know her opinion.

'Yeah. Point number 1- I guess he believed he was not worthy enough to ask your hand. Point number 2- He needed that time away from you to figure himself out. You know it can be scary when you are so influenced by someone that you may lose yourself in the process.'

I took a deep breath and stared out the bus window as we crossed Vizag. I was feeling overwhelmed by everything happening around me. I couldn't believe that I travelled all this distance to find out about him and it worked! When I told my dad that I was going to do this I didn't expect this is what I'll find out. I didn't expect to feel extremely special and loved and what an amazing guy I was in love with. I thought I should give him that space if that's what he needed. I'm ready to do that. I waited a year not knowing what was going to happen. I can wait for another, knowing his love and cherishing it.

Chapter-13

My dad was waiting at the bus stop to pick me up. He took my bag and placed it in front of him and asked me to hop on. I waved at Adi and Akanksha and we started home. On the way, my dad asked the question he had been waiting to ask me,

'So? What happened in Vizag? Did you find out anything?'

I smiled and almost yelled against the wind hitting my face, 'He loves me back!'

'I'm going to need more than that Kanna. Why did he leave?' He asked while we waited at the signal.

'He loved and admired me so much that he got inspired to take things seriously and turned his life around...'

'Well... Okay. I still think he shouldn't have left you hanging. He should have had the courage to break it off directly.' The traffic moved as the signal blinked green and I began to yell again.

'That's the whole point, Nanna. He didn't want to break it off. He probably wanted me then more than ever. He just didn't know how to ask.' My dad had been quiet for the rest of the ride.

'So, what are you going to do now?' He asked as we got off the bike. I took a deep breath and with a lot of confidence and peace, I said, 'I'll wait for him to return Nanna. I'm sure he will.'

'Hmmm... Okay. You look happier. So, I guess I need to make peace with it too.' I blushed and nodded.

The next few weeks went by preparing for the jury and exams. Akanksha and my study sessions now became a group of three. Aditya fit perfectly well in our routine and we motivated each other to do better. I improved my grades from the last semester and needed to do much better in the finals to cover the average score.

After the exams, I spent some time at my grandmother's place. Adi and Akanksha got to spend more time together with me out of the picture. They played badminton often and went on dates. Adi wanted to pursue a Master's in CEPT college in Ahmedabad so he started preparing. Even though that wasn't her initial plan, Akanksha jumped at the opportunity to spend time with Adi and get a Master's degree. I applied as an intern at a few major jewellery stores in Hyderabad and Bangalore.

I got accepted into four of the five stores I applied for but one email caught my eye and attention more than the others.

...We are glad to accept your application as a Junior Designer at Mangalore Jewels, JP Nagar, Bangalore...

I was elated. I jumped up and ran into the hall to tell my mom the good news.

'Maa...!!! I got accepted.' I hugged her.

'Wow, awesome Kanna. I'm so proud of you. Which one?'

'Mangalore jewels. Yay!' My mom's face dropped and her smile faded. 'Bangalore?' she asked.

'Yes... Maa it's a wonderful opportunity.'

'But it's so far away. We live in a metropolitan city too! You can get a job here. Statistically, Hyderabad has a lot more Jewellery shops than Bangalore.'

'What? No. You are just making that up Maa. It's just a matter of one year. Please. Don't say no.' She thought about it for a while but seeing how confident I looked and sounded she finally gave in and said, 'But only on one condition. You need to stay at our relative's place or at least close to them.'

'Abba Maa...! I can't do that. Listen I'm an independent and strong woman. I can handle things on my own. I will look for a small studio apartment near the store itself.' She rolled her eyes and muttered under her breath, *this girl never listens to a word I say.* I smiled to myself and went into the room to share the news with Akanksha. She said,

'Whoa, Bangalore huh? So, I'm thinking this is intentional?'

'What do you mean?'

'I mean... It's Bangalore! You are going there because it's Subhash's city. Tell me I'm wrong?'

'Well... No, and yes. I mean it did cross my mind that he lived there and all but he isn't there now, is he? And Dude, you know it. This will be a great start to my career. Don't you think?'

'Yeah, that's true. Anyway, I'm so proud of you Varna. You have risen back up like a phoenix. I'm glad you decided to pursue Subhash and we went to Vizag.'

'Haha. Thank you and so am I... proud of you.'

Later I called my dad. He said,

'Super proud of you madam. When are we going?'

'When are WE going? No. I'm going.'

'Yeah, I mean we will come to settle you down first. When shall we start?'

'Nanna I can look up places in Google and I can figure it out.'

'Of course, you can Kanna. But you don't need to. You can't say no to this If you want to go to Bangalore.' He gave an ultimatum.

'Okay... They mentioned I can start at the beginning of July. So, we have 20 days. Whenever you are free. Let's go and figure out my living situation.'

'Yeah. That's my girl. I'll check my calendar and we'll finalize a date.'

The next weekend, which happened to be a long weekend, Mom, Dad and I headed to Bangalore. My mom insisted she would come too. We booked a hotel near JP Nagar and checked in. We made a beautiful vacation out of this weekend trip. On the first day, we walked to the store and searched every street around it so we can find a place to stay within walking distance. We did come across a few apartments which were not in my budget range so we decided to spread the radius of our search. After roaming almost all day we finally got a small 1bhk apartment which was perfect in every way possible.

As we entered the door, there was an open kitchen facing the hall and towards the right, there was a balcony facing the road. There was one bedroom with an attached bathroom. It had plenty of light and ventilation. It was around 1.2 km from my place of work and was located in a good residential area. The owner left for a temporary 2-year job in the US so some of the furniture was still there. There was a small 2+1-seater sofa set and a bed. Mom and Dad were also very happy with the place. We confirmed it and paid a little advance and booked the place for the whole of next year. We went and had a relaxing dinner in a nearby restaurant and slept in.

The next morning, we put on tourist shoes and visited so many places around the city. First, we went to the ISKCON Temple, then visited the Lalbagh botanical gardens and ended the day with some street shopping on MG Road. My dad declared that Hyderabad was a lot better compared to Bangalore, traffic-wise. My mom loved the city and the greenery. At one point she even told me she envies me that I get to do this exploring. The next day, we checked out of the hotel and headed to the Phoenix Mall. We had an afternoon flight back to Hyderabad so we thought we could visit the mall, have lunch and head to the airport.

We were astonished by the vastness and the grandeur of the place. It took us one hour to even enter the mall after knowing that we were near it. We placed our bags in the cloakroom and proceeded inside. We clicked a lot of pictures. As I was checking my phone to see if the pictures were good enough to post on Facebook, I heard someone call out my mom's name. My mom got so excited and hugged the woman. My view was blocked by moving people and my parents. Once they exchanged greetings, my mom turned back to call me to greet the woman. The minute I saw her, I froze. Aunty came closer and said,

'Varna...!! How are you? You have grown up into a beautiful woman now.'

It was Kavitha Aunty. Subhash's mother. My future mother-in-law! My heart started beating recklessly faster. I couldn't form a sentence. I nervously smiled at her and awkwardly said, 'Hello Aunty. I'm fine. Thank you.' My dad was looking at me and smiling naughtily. My tension began to grow. I raised my eyebrows and warned him not to say anything but he didn't listen to me. He asked Aunty,

'So, Kavitha. How's Subhash doing? I heard he is doing a Master's in the US?'

'Yes, Prakash. That came as a shock to me too. He decided in his final year that he would want to start a Business. Until then the plan was always to finish studies and come back to Bangalore. If he gets a job in placements from the college, well and good. If not, he was supposed to work at Murali's company. Hey by the way... You said your flight was at 4 30pm, so what's your plan for lunch?' I widened my eyes dreading the next thing that she was going to say.

'We were supposed to have lunch here and head to the airport.' My mom said.

'No. Your plan has changed now. Let's go home. You can meet Murali too. We shall have lunch there, just like in old times. We will drop you at the airport later. Come on now, don't say no. My house is just 20 mins away.' I started pulling my mom's dress hinting her to back out but she didn't bother me and agreed to the plan. I closed my eyes tightly and sighed. Kavitha Aunty and Mom started walking together. My dad put an arm on my shoulder and asked,

'Hello, madam. What happened to you? Why are you shying away?'

'Nanna... I'm not shying away. It is just so sudden and overwhelming. I mean she is going to be my mother-in-law! The last time I saw her I was just a silly little 11-year-old who hated her for taking my best friend away from me. Now...

I'm in love with her son... I don't know. Do you think she knows about us?'

'Kanna. I guess you are thinking too much. You didn't even talk to Subhash yet. You don't know what your future holds. Don't build on...' I was now pissed at my dad. I stopped walking and gave him a death glare. 'Sorry. I mean don't look at her as your "mother-in-law" yet. She was someone who loved you so much for what you were and you loved her back. She used to bring your favourite food all the time. She always encouraged you and believed in you more than she did in her son. Just look at her that way. Please put this whole Subhash episode on pause for now. Can you do that?'

'Yeah. I guess... Okay. Thanks, Nanna.'

'Yeah. She always believed you would achieve something special in life. Now that I think of it, you achieved grabbing her son. And helped him to get his life together.' I gasped at that comment and looked at my dad wide-mouthed. He was laughing. I kicked him on his arm and said, 'Stop saying that. I didn't do anything.' And I kept blushing the entire way to their house.

As her car slowed down, I looked up at the house. It was a beautiful modern villa with granite claddings and pergola and a garden. The entrance was grand with a huge teak wood door as long as the ceiling. My dad got down the car before me and came to my door. While I was getting down, he said, 'Well you have always wanted a house with a huge open area to develop a garden. There it is. Subhash is their only son, so...'

'Oh my god, Nanna...! Stop it. You asked me to not think about it but you are rubbing it in my face now.'

'Haha. I'm glad about this match. I would totally approve.' He said still smiling. I thought it was cute so I didn't say anything. As we were walking through the driveway to the entrance, I kept seeing visions of Subhash growing up in this house. I thought to myself *He must have played cricket here all the time! He loved the rain so he must have sat on these stairs and enjoyed the rain.*

The interiors of the house were sophisticated. Completely modern style architecture. A huge hall with double height and a skylight on top. The house had hanging steps made of wood. They had a huge pooja room. Aunty showed us a room to put our luggage and freshen up if we wanted. We went into what looked like a guest room and sat there for a bit. Meanwhile, Murali uncle came down and greeted all of us. They had a cook. Aunty gave her some instructions and came back with juice glasses. We all had some juice and got to talking. Uncle asked me how and what I was doing.

'I did Bachelors of Arts uncle. My goal is to become a jewellery designer so I applied for an internship here in Mangalore Jewels, JP Nagar. I would be starting from the first of next month.'

'Oh wow. Wonderful Beta. I was always so sure about your career. I knew you would kill it whatever you took up. You are a rockstar.'

'Oh no, Uncle. It's nothing.' I said modestly.

'I'm glad to say our Subhash has also chosen a good path for himself. He was pretty clueless until even two years ago. Then something happened in the last year at Gitam's. He suddenly shifted gears and decided on a path that was perfect for him. I'm super proud of him.' My heart swelled with pride hearing that. I knew it would make Subhash happy. I wanted to tell him this when we start talking again. Aunty interrupted and said, 'Okay enough boasting about our kids now. Shall we talk about what's with you guys...' she said and the conversation went into my parent's jobs, their work situation and other things like that. Meanwhile, I started looking around the house admiring its perfection. Just then Aunty said, 'You like it beta? Subhash got it all designed and constructed very particularly to his taste. Why don't you go around and have a tour?' She said and she summoned a maid who was standing at the corner all the while. 'Take madam upstairs and show her around.' She said to her. I knew my dad was smiling at me but I didn't look at him for the fear of me blushing again.

The maid took me to the first floor. She showed me the master bedroom, the home theatre and the family lounge. I asked her what was upstairs. She said there was only one room and a terrace and it was Subhash's room. My heartbeat started raising. The curiosity was killing me. I asked her if it was unlocked. She said yes and I went upstairs. When she was about to follow me, I turned around and said I'd be fine. So, she stayed back. Every step I was taking I started feeling closer to him. I stood in front of his door, holding the door knob. I closed my eyes, controlled my breathing and opened the door. I gasped looking at the room.

His room was like a small condo in itself. Probably because he wasn't living there, it was very neat and spotless. It was in shades of grey. There was a central area with a huge black/white portrait of just his face, smiling, right in front of the door. It had a grey sofa below it. Towards the left, there was an elevated area on which there was a huge king-size bed with black covers and a curtain behind the bed. The elevated area had different flooring and towards both sides, there were closets with black and white design. One of the doors was a little lower than the others which I imagined to be the entrance to his attached bathroom. Towards the right side of the room, there was a small space with dumbbells and other workout stuff. That side of the wall had photo frames of some of his fav food items, ironically, which made me laugh. Towards the other corner, there was a platform on which there was an oven, a coffee machine and a few crockery sets. All in black or grey keeping in tone with the rest of the room. The entire wall on the third side was covered with blinds, again grey in colour. I walked towards that side and opened the blinds and held on to my chest, laughing. It opened into a balcony which further opened into the terrace. The balcony had wooden tiles and a fan on the roof. It even had a couple of potted plants here and there. There was a bean bag on one side and a black wicker swing on the other side. There were posters of King Kohli and MS Dhoni on the wall, both in black/white. The terrace had an artificial lawn and pots all along the parapet. Towards the other side of the terrace, there was a pergola with a granite seat. It had creepers all over the top giving it a beautiful romantic vibe. I felt spellbound. It was like a dream. So stunning and perfect.

I walked around the terrace for a bit and sat on the granite seat. Later I walked back into the room and went to his portrait. It was so huge and felt so damn real. Every other noise around me suddenly faded and I could hear my heartbeat. I went a little closer. I looked into his eyes and then his lips. Without me realizing my fingers started touching the portrait. Like I desperately wanted it to be him, to feel him, hug him and kiss him. I bent forward and kissed his face. Then I went to his bed and sat on it and felt the bedsheet. Its satin silk finish felt so soft against my hands. I grabbed a pillow and hugged it tightly smelling it. I looked up and saw the bathroom door. I went inside and was pleasantly surprised, yet again. It had a huge mirror with a huge black basin. He had a black toothbrush too. There was a shower area with black granite tiles. It was beautiful. Suddenly I was distracted by a phone call. It was from Akanksha. I lifted the call and before I could say anything she asked, 'So did you find a place? How's Bangalore?'

'Dude... Guess where I am right now.' I said with all the excitement in the world showing in my voice.

'Whoa. You sound... elated. Where are you?'

'Subhash's bedroom!' It sounded like she choked on whatever she was drinking. 'What...!!!???' She exclaimed. 'Why and How on Earth?'

'We met Kavitha Aunty at the mall and she invited us to her house.'

'That sounds crazy! So how is it?'

'Surprisingly beautiful. It is all black and white, coordinated perfectly from the bedsheets to the crockery and beautifully maintained. I'm amazed.'

'Wow. Okay... How are you feeling?'

'I never want to leave this place. If Subhash was here, I don't think I'll have the heart to step out of this room.'

'Cool. Okay then. I'll call you later. Just called to find out when are you going to be back.'

'Our flight is at 4:30 pm. We are still on for tomorrow's lunch. I remember. Adi's birthday. I'm there don't worry.'

I cut the call and put my phone back. I felt my lipstick in the bag and I got an idea. I opened my lipstick and wrote on the mirror... I WAS HERE and drew a heart beside it. As I came out of the room, I got a message from my dad saying lunch was ready and they were calling me downstairs.

I put the phone inside, looked at his portrait and said, 'I'll see you soon Mister.'

We finished lunch, talking about how we used to spend time back when they were in Hyderabad. Aunty went on and on about Subhash and how well he was doing in college, which I couldn't get enough of. It was lovely to know all these things and I felt super proud of him. Uncle asked me so many questions about my new job and where I was staying. He also offered to drop by anytime I want. When we finished, I helped Aunty clean up the table. Just then I saw her phone ringing. She was carrying some dishes in her hand so she asked me to see who called. Before I could get to her phone and check, the call was missed and the screen opened to the last used app. It was Subhash's chat on WhatsApp. I couldn't help but notice his display picture. It was him standing on the lawn beside this long wall with the name 'University of Pennsylvania'. I clicked on it and it opened contact information. I saw his phone number there and read it to myself a couple of times. I had the urge to click on it, call him and listen to his voice. I was craving it. I quickly opened my phone and saved his contact. I finished helping her and we all sat in the living room chitchatting. Aunty later dropped us at the airport and we came to Hyderabad.

Chapter- 14

The next afternoon Akanksha, Adi and I went to a restaurant to celebrate Adi's birthday. The only thing I could talk about was Subhash and his beautiful, huge house and his dreamy bedroom. After listening to me brag about him for about half an hour, Aditya finally asked, 'Are you planning on texting him? I heard you "stole" his number from his mom.' I looked at Akanksha, a little surprised that she told him. She shrugged and smiled.

'Hmmm, I don't know Adi. I want to. But I don't know if I should. I heard Aunty say he is coming to India in two months.'

'That's great. You can meet him then.' For the rest of the lunch, we talked about them and their plans and at the end, we cut a cake for Adi.

That night I was rolling on the bed not able to sleep. I kept thinking about Subhash and the days when we used to text and call. It was so exciting and I felt the urge to do that again. Now we both are different people. We have been through a lot and what we feel for each other is a lot deeper and more meaningful and romantic. I wanted to hear him tell me that he loves me. I opened WhatsApp and zoomed in on his profile picture to get a better look at him. He was wearing a black jacket, grey jeans and black shoes and had sunglasses on. But his smile was dominating the picture. His beautiful, pleasant smile melted my heart. I started typing... *Hey Subhash... It's me Varna* and then I erased it. I tried multiple things but nothing seemed right. I was not even sure if I should text him. Finally, I decided to go for it.

V: Subhash... Varna here... Can we talk?

Suddenly his status showed 'online'. My heart started pounding. This is real. It's not a dream or a fantasy. The message reached him and he saw it. HE SAW IT. I started feeling nervous. It's been 45 seconds and still no response. My body started to shiver just like when I used to have panic attacks. I started to doubt everything that had happened for the last few months. *What if he moved on? What if everything that I was building all these days was nothing but a lie? What if he meant it when he said this is it for us?* I started to sweat badly so I threw the phone on the bed and went running into the balcony. I looked up and kept taking deep breaths until my body was back to normal and then I went back to the bedroom. I was looking at the phone lying on my bed upside down, dreading to see it. Just then my phone started to ring. I looked at it and it was him! Subhash was calling...! I let out a sigh and lifted the call.

'Hello, Varna?' My body started to settle down. It felt like I was being released from a grip and I collapsed onto the bed. I couldn't say a word. It was too emotional. I pressed the phone against my ear to hear his melodic voice again.

'Varna... You there?'

'Yes...I'm here.' I said with a happy laughing sigh.

'Oh my god Varna... Would you believe me if I said I missed you? I missed talking to you. I missed hearing your voice and feeling the love you have for me?' His voice was shaking. This was the first time we were talking to each other in more capacity than a friend. I felt love. I felt his pain. I felt all the comfort in the world knowing we are talking again.

'Yes. Would you believe me if I said I have been craving to hear from you all this while?' There was silence...

'Varna... I was really stupid to do that to you. I'm sorry. I have regretted it every second of every day ever since. I shouldn't have left at all. I miss you so much, baby...' A smile pushed through my cheeks hearing him call me 'baby'.

'No. You have gone to study! It was for your career. I understand that. But breaking up with me...yeah that you should regret.' I said playfully.

'I do Varna. I would do anything to repair that situation. What do you want me to do? I'm all yours.'

'Make it up to me. You are going to have to persuade me.'

'Oh, I sure will... Urgh I missed you, baby. I can't say that enough. I'm so glad you texted me. How did you get my number?'

'Well, that's a long story.'

'I have got all the time in the world for you. Tell me.'

'Hmmm... Not now Subhash.'

'Varna... I understand that you are angry with me...' The vibe of the call completely changed. I loved that we were back on talking terms again but I couldn't not think about the past two years.

'What were you doing all this while Subhash? Where were you? If you regretted it so much, why didn't you try to talk to me again?'

'Okay, the truth Varna? I was feeling guilty. I was torn to see you cry. I was devastated to have left you like that. I should have done something. But every time I think of contacting you again it pained me. I remember how you bawled after you read the letter. I remember how much you wanted to make this work. But I left. I felt silly and I could never get over that guilt. I thought I was leaving for a good reason. I wanted to make myself worthy of you. I didn't believe that you would want to stay with someone like me. But I was wrong. I thought I loved you and admired you but I realized you loved me too! I shouldn't have left you hanging that way. I'm sorry Varna.' His original strong beautiful voice felt weak and vulnerable and all the anger I felt didn't seem enough to put him through that.

'Subhash... Nothing can stop me from being with you. We are meant to be together and I will fight this world if I have to, to reach you.'

'Varna... I don't know what to say. You are too amazing. You are brilliant and beautiful, ambitious and determined, caring and loving. I don't know if I deserve you. But I would strive my entire life to make myself worthy of you. I never want to leave you again baby.'

I just smiled and bit my lower lip, blushing.

'Did you just smile? God, you're killing me. I want to see you Varna. Can we do a video call?'

'Hold on Mister. Not now. I want to see you too. But not like this. I will meet you directly. Very soon.'

'Wow! I'm coming to India in two months. I will come to Hyderabad to meet you.'

'That would be lovely.' I said, planning to surprise him in Bangalore.

'Oh, by the way, what did you mean when you said, you saw me cry?' I asked, confused.

'I was there Varna...'

'What...!? What did you see? Why didn't you come and meet me then?'

'I came to Hyderabad to meet you on your birthday. I came to your college with my friend Madhu. When I was walking towards the main building, I saw you walking towards the canteen, so I followed you. I saw the surprise your classmates gave you and I thought it was really sweet. I wanted to meet you and leave as quickly as possible but after that surprise, I didn't want to see you and tell you that I'm leaving. I knew that would upset you. So, I waited outside. I kept thinking about what this could mean and how you would react. My confidence was dropping every second. I was way too vulnerable to say anything to your face. So, when I heard the bell ring, I sat down and wrote that letter to you, right there. Madhu was begging me to not put him in that situation. But I had to. I saw you take the box and go into the canteen and then you came back out to call me and then you got the letter and read it under that tree and you cried. I was right behind you Varna.'

I didn't respond. I was reliving the whole episode in my head. *He was there?* No wonder that guy Madhu kept looking behind my back.

'Say something, baby.' His words brought me back to the present. What happened was past. Now I have him. We are talking again. This is the beginning of something new. I didn't want to spoil that for myself and him.

'Subhash... I don't have anything to say about it. I don't care anymore. Let's just forget the whole thing even happened, okay?'

'...Okay if that's what you want... Anyway, how is college? Are you almost done?'

'Yeah, almost done. I applied for an internship and I'll be starting work next month.'

'That's great. I'm proud of you Varna.' I inhaled deeply and closed my eyes. I slowly rested my head on the pillow. I was hearing him breathe. Just the presence, even if it was virtual, gave me a sense of security and comfort. I just held the phone to my ear and went to sleep to the rhythm of his breath.

The next morning when I woke up, I worried it might have been a dream, so I opened WhatsApp to check if Subhash did come back into my life. There were a few unread messages from last night.

S: Varna...! Oh my God. Of course, we can. Can I call you now?

S: Hey? You there?

And a few from five minutes ago too.

S: Good morning, Baby. Did you sleep well last night?

I smiled and replied,

V: The best... What time is it for you?

S: It's around 9:30 pm. I just had dinner.

V: Okay... I just woke up. I don't have much to do today. Work will start in another ten days. Until then it's holiday time!

S: Wow. I wish I was there Varna. I'm dying to meet you.

V: Hmmm me too! Let me freshen up and come. I'll call you. Is that okay? What time do you sleep usually?

S: Doesn't matter. Call me.

As I finished my morning routine, Dad was almost ready to leave for the office. I was too excited to not share the good news with him. I sat beside him at the breakfast table and said, 'Guess who I was talking to last night?'

'Who? Tell me...'

'Subhash... Nanna I texted him. He is extremely happy that I did. So am I! And we...' I hesitated a little bit, 'We got back together Nanna.'

'That's wonderful Kanna. I'm happy for you. But are you sure about this? Him?'

'Surer than I have been about anything else in my life Nanna. I love him and so does he. We are meant to be together.' My dad smiled and put his hand on my head like he was blessing me. He suddenly called out to my mom and yelled,

'Geetha...! They are back. Subhash called her last night.' I opened my mouth wide in utter shock and looked at my dad.

'Nanna! What are you doing?' My mom came out of the kitchen looking happy. She looked at me and put her hand on her waist and said,

'You thought I didn't know? Nanna told me everything. Why could you not tell me Kanna?' I stared at my dad with folded hands.

'What...!? She forced it out of me.' My mom came around the table and hugged my head from behind.

'I don't know why you felt the need to hide it from me Varna. But whatever it is, I'm happy for you. I love that guy. Kavitha is a good friend. It would be lovely to see you as her daughter-in-law.'

'That's exactly why Maa. I know how much Kavitha Aunty and her friendship meant to you. I felt you might be upset with them if you knew the reason for my panic attacks was Subhash.'

'Well... Of course, I was upset. But I always thought about how great it would be if you guys were together. So, my manifestation worked.'

'Haha Yup. Your manifestation it was.' I said sarcastically. I was going into my room when something suddenly struck me.

'Does Kavitha aunty know?' I asked my mom.

'...I don't know. We didn't discuss anything because as of two days ago, you were still broken up. But I felt she knew by the way she spoke about you.' I raised my eyebrows and thought to myself... *Lovely!*

I went back inside and settled in my chair and called Subhash.

'Hey, baby. I was waiting for your call. What's up?'

'Okay, what's with this "baby"? It's so weird hearing you say that.'

'What...!? I thought you like it. It just comes naturally anyway. I love it.'

'Hmmm... I like it.' I said, blushing. 'By the way, our families know our entire situation, you know that?'

'What? How? I didn't tell anyone.'

'I told my dad. My dad told my mom. She thinks your mom knows it too.'

'No way. I'm sure my mom doesn't know anything. I casually mentioned I was talking to you back when we were together. That's it.'

'She must have guessed it. Your voice oozes out love when you talk about me.'

'Haha, it's that evident huh?'

'Yes...So tell me about your life there. How's Pennsylvania? How far is it from New York? Did you visit?'

'I'm mostly around campus. But yeah, I did get to travel quite a bit. I found great travel buddies here. Why are you interested in New York specifically?'

'What do you mean why? It's only like my favourite city ever! It's where *Friends* happen. I love that show. It's my dream vacation.'

'That's my favourite show too! And yes, I have been there. It's surreal.'

We talked about so many other things for about two hours until he was tired to form full sentences. Then he went to sleep.

Chapter-15

I told Subhash that I got a job but didn't mention that it was in Bangalore. So, I had to lie to him about what I was doing and why I was busy while hectically packing to move to another city. We have been talking almost every day since the day I texted him. Some days more than others. We were completely obsessed with each other. Everything started to feel better, sound better, look better. My Dopamine and oxytocin levels were so high that I started feeling more creative. I began work for my own brand of jewellery and started sketching multiple ideas. He was studying hard for his exams.

The day I was moving to Bangalore came in no time and my mom was a lot more emotional than usual. While we were about to start, she said,

'Kanna. This is the first time that you are going to be on your own. Please take care of yourself. Keep calling me every day...' with tears in her eyes.

'Maa... I'll be absolutely fine... Please don't cry!'

'Yeah, of course. You have always been a very sorted woman which we take great pride in. But the world out there is not as colourful and beautiful as you tend to see it. You need to be more careful.'

'I will be. Don't worry, ma'am. Now shall we start? We don't want to miss our flight now, do we?'

'I wish Subhash was there in Bangalore... I would have worried a lot less.'

I smiled at that comment and hugged her tightly and said,

'Maa. I can take care of myself. Also, he'll be in Bangalore in another month.'

'Okay...All the best Kanna.' She said and waved at me while I left for the airport with my dad.

Dad stayed with me for three days to help me set up the place initially. He helped me clean the apartment, put new sheets on my bed and we went to utensils shopping. He dropped me off at my work on the first day and got acquainted with the route I would be taking to reach work. He spoke to my boss and then headed over to the airport.

That night after work I came back to the house and looked around. That was the first time I ever had a place of my own completely to myself. I took a nice long shower and settled down with the pizza I ordered. Just as I was about to have it, I got a call from Kavitha Aunty.

'Hello, Aunty... How are you?'

'Hi, Varna. I'm good. How was your first day? Made any friends?'

'Not yet Aunty... I met all the co-workers today. Yet to start real work.'

'Amma called me in the morning. She told me you would be joining today. She also mentioned that this was the first time you were living alone.'

'Yes, Aunty. But I'm fine. I just ordered food and I'm about to eat.'

'Good. Have fun maa. Do remember that I'm here for anything you need. You can call me up any time. And you can drop by the house anytime too.'

'Sure Aunty... Thank you.'

I was pleasantly surprised to receive a call from her. That night when Subhash called, I told him all about my new job, the people I met and the workplace and everything. I was so tempted to tell him that I was in Bangalore but I wanted to surprise him, so I restrained myself.

Finally, the day came when Subhash was landing in Bangalore. I imagined multiple ways to surprise him but every one of them needed the involvement of his parents. I wanted to pick him up from the airport but obviously, Aunty and Uncle were going to do that and me being there would raise so many questions. And I didn't know what Subhash has or has not been telling them. That night I understood how long a minute or sixty seconds can be. I lay on my bed looking at my phone and counting the minutes when he would enter the city. I couldn't sleep as I kept imagining what he must be doing at that moment. The phone finally pinged with the most awaited message.

S: Varna... Babe, I'm here! Landed 20mins ago. Please go to sleep if you haven't. I'll text you in the morning.

V: Hey. Yes, I'm awake. Waiting for your message.

S: I'm so excited to see you soon babe. I'll figure out when I can make it to Hyderabad and I'll let you know. We are just 600kms away. I know it's far but feels very close to me.

We are just 6 km away... And it kills me to not be in your arms yet.

V: Yeah. I'm going to sleep now. I'll talk to you tomorrow. Goodnight Subhash.

I felt sad that I didn't figure out a way to surprise him yet. Waiting around seemed much sadder so I decided I would call him in the morning and just tell him so that we can meet as early as possible.

I woke up early the next morning around 6 am, feeling restless. As I was not able to go back to sleep, I freshened up, fixed my t-shirt and shorts and poured myself a fresh cup of coffee. I needed some peace from the madness I was feeling yesterday so I tied my hair into a messy bun, took my coffee and went to the balcony. I stood there leaning over the parapet, sipping coffee and breathing the fresh morning oxygen. Just then, I noticed someone standing on the opposite side of the road, leaning on his Royal Enfield, folding his arms and staring at me. I was perplexed by the resemblance. I stood tall and looked keenly at him. He looked a lot like Subhash.

There he was... Subhash... In-person... Right there!

At first, I couldn't believe it was him. I was convinced that I have gone completely crazy and started seeing him there but then I realized it was him when he smiled at me. I let out a heavy sigh and smiled back at him. My heart rate became erratic when he stood up straight and put both his hands in his pockets. I couldn't help but notice how stylish he looked. I left my coffee on the parapet and ran downstairs and rapidly jumped into his arms. He hugged me back so tightly and slowly landed me on the floor. That's when I noticed how tall he has grown from the last time I saw him.

'What the hell are you doing here? I still can't believe it is you... Subhash.' I yelled with excitement, still hugging him.

'Varna...' He said, holding my face in his palms and gaining my complete undivided attention, 'I love you.'

Those words passed right through the ears and hit directly to the heart like an arrow. I had goosebumps all over my body. I felt his love and his longing in those words. My love felt so small compared to what I saw in his eyes at that moment. I couldn't say it back because I felt nothing could do justice to what we were feeling. I looked deep into his eyes, nodded my head sideways and hugged him again. This hug was gentler and more present. I felt every inch of his body that I was touching and absorbed him into me. After a while, he broke the silence and said,

'Well... Seems like you didn't grow much taller after I left Hyderabad. You are still the same height.'

I gasped at that comment, immediately released the hug and started hitting on his arm. Then I heard the most beautiful sound on the entire planet, his laughter. It was so genuine and heartful. I smiled to myself hearing that and observing his face while he laughed. It was perfection.

'You seem like 3 inches taller than me, that's all.' I said defensively.

'What...!? I thought you were smart. I'm easily 6 inches taller, see.' He said standing beside me and measuring how tall he was. My head stopped at his shoulder. I pushed him away and rolled my eyes.

He looked up at my balcony and said, 'Your coffee must have gotten cold. Can I take you out for some coffee?'

'Like this!?' I said pointing at myself. I was wearing thigh-length shorts and a dirty T-shirt with a messy bun.

'You look absolutely gorgeous to me! Beauty like no other.' He said, inhaling and looking deeply into me. We both looked into each other's eyes for a few seconds and then I shook my head and said,

'Let me change and come. We'll go out.'

We went to a small coffee shop nearby; he ordered tea and I ordered coffee.

'Okay so now tell me. How do you know I'm here? And how long were you waiting for me to come out of that balcony?'

'I texted Akanksha.' I was surprised. 'I saw the note you left for me on my bathroom mirror and I was...in shock. I thought about it for a while and guessed it must be you but it was all so confusing. You didn't tell me you came to Bangalore. Then I imagined you didn't, probably to surprise me. But I was too restless and anxious so I searched for Akanksha on Facebook and found her. Luckily, she was online and she replied. I told her I wanted to meet you as soon as I can. She hesitated but then gave up your address. I would have rushed immediately but then I didn't want to disturb your sleep so, I sneaked out in the morning.'

'Wow...' is all I could say. Just then our orders came in. I sipped my coffee still putting all the pieces together. He continued.

'So, I know that your internship is here but how were you at my house?'

'Aunty met us at Phoenix Mall when Amma, Nanna and I came here to search for an apartment for me and invited us for lunch.'

'Huh... Okay.' He said sipping his tea and enjoying it.

'By the way, your room is such a masterpiece dude. I didn't know you loved black so much. I couldn't come out of the room.'

Later he dropped me back home and left. As I saw his figure fade, I started feeling my chest tighten up and sweat forming all over my body. Soon I was struggling to breathe. I was instantly distracted by a phone call from Akanksha. I slowly felt the pressure being released. After controlling my breathing pattern, I exhaled and lifted the call. She sounded more excited than I was. She asked me if Subhash has turned up. I told her all about the surprise and the date and thanked her for being a crucial part of one of the most beautiful moments of my life.

Chapter-16

After seeing Subhash come and pick me up post work almost every day for 10 days now, all my colleagues got used to him. Some of them know him by name and makes small talk now and then too. We have been roaming around the city on his Royal Enfield and exploring various food joints every evening. I saw how passionate and observant he was about the food business. He gave me a lot of trivia about different kinds of street food. That was more information about food than I have learnt in the entire 22 years of my life.

We went to the school where he had the rest of his education after he left Hyderabad. He showed me how his life was after he came to Bangalore. He took me to his intermediate college too. We spoke about his friends, my friends and everything in between. He took me to the ground where he played his first-ever Cricket league match. He talked passionately about the game.

We went to the movie *Aaha kalyanam*, Nani's latest release. I talked about him so much and made him realize the phenomenon that is Nani and ultimately turned him into a Nani fan too.

I sometimes had symptoms of my panic attacks come and go but I was clueless as to why. Previously I was convinced it was because Subhash left that I had those attacks. But now, he was right here, with me. I figured to wait it out and observe if it goes any further to take any kind of action against them. But other than that, life had been amazing.

One evening when he picked me up, he took me directly to my apartment and stopped the bike.

'Do you have to go somewhere?' I asked, getting off the bike, confused.

'Yes. If you agree, I would like to take you on a special date.'

'A date? That's intriguing. But why are we here then?'

'Because... It's a surprise. We have been conquering the city all these days and exploring so much like the best friends we were back then. But today is about my girlfriend. I think I waited too long to hear you say it and I want to push you a little more.' I wanted to tell him *I love you* for a very long time now. I planned to say it directly to him on my birthday but he left. Even after we got together, he told me that he loves me almost 250 times but I never repeated the words and I knew he was waiting to hear them.

'I'll tell you when I feel it. Today is not the day. You deserve to take the punishment for a few more days.' I said, almost like a challenge.

'Well... Then I'm ready to prove you wrong. It is 5:45 pm now. I'll come and pick you up right here at 7:30. Wear this dress and wait here for me.' He said handing me a paper bag and riding off. I went upstairs smiling, hugging the bag close.

It was a sleeveless dark pink knee-length frock with pleats from below the chest. He also gave me a set of beautiful gold looped earrings that would go perfectly well with the dress. I always admired his sense of style but I adored his taste in the clothes he picked for me. I loved how he was bribing me with all these to hear me say that I love him. I was loving to see him wait.

I took a shower, blow-dried my hair, waxed my hands and legs, painted my nails and put on a little makeup. The dress fit perfectly well on my body and I stood in front of the mirror appreciating my beauty. The dress gave me a feeling of seeing myself through his eyes and I loved it. As I finished dressing up, selecting a pair of sandals and a bag for the dress, I heard a car horn. I frowned and went into the balcony, putting on my earrings. He got out of his mom's car and waved at me. He was wearing semi-formal brown shirt and black trousers and looked stunning.

I nodded my head signalling that I was impressed. He stretched out both his hands and bent down in a bow. I laughed and signalled that I'd be down in 5 minutes. As I was crossing the road he came towards the passenger seat of the car, handed me a box of Ferrero Rocher chocolates and opened the door for me.

'Wow. A special date indeed... What is this about?'

'Come on get in. We have reservations.'

'Ooooh interesting...'

As he sat in the driver's seat and started the car he said,

'I'm going to have a very tough time concentrating on the road with you looking like that.' I blushed and turned my head towards the window trying to hide the smile. I sensed he was looking at me. He laughed slightly and started the car. He specifically picked out the most romantic songs of the past decade to play on the Bluetooth, humming to them. The whole ride there was a lot of sexual tension between us. Every time he had his hand on the gear rod, I was tempted to touch him. He would sense it and smile at me and I would just blush and turn away. Just as he was taking a turn into the parking of JW Marriott, I looked at him and said,

'Okay... I get it. You are rich!' He laughed and ignored my comment. 'Subhash... I have never been to such places before. Are you sure about this?'

'What is 'such places' Varna... It's just a restaurant. Come on.' He said getting down the car and coming towards my door. I took a deep breath and took up on the offer to hold his hand as we walked towards the elevator. We went to the terrace restaurant; *Spice Terrace* and I was completely in awe of the place. It was a mildly breezy night giving us the most romantic vibes. He took us to the best table with candle lights beside the pool. We sat across each other and it took me a few seconds to adjust to the grandeur. I was looking around, the tables, the people, the waiters, the food, the ambience, the aromas and the breeze... it was all so special. Just then I realized he has been staring at me all this while. We have been so comfortable and easy all these days but today everything was different. I couldn't look him in the eye so I kept avoiding it. The smile never left my face and I was biting my upper lip and looking for the waiter. He then held both my hands and said,

'Varna... Look at me.' One second into those eyes and I couldn't move my eyes anywhere else. His eyes pierced through my face and touched deeply into my soul. The effect was hypnotizing. He left my hands and fell back onto the chair. I couldn't help but admire his perfect features in the romantic lighting. He was glowing. I don't know for how long we stared into each other like that but we were distracted by the waiter who came to take the order. I inhaled sharply and fell back too, like I just came out of the hypnotization.

The food was delicious. We had a wonderful meal, catching glances and talking through the eyes. Our souls spoke to each other and danced to the music of our hearts. We made little conversation directly but almost towards the end of the meal I shook my head sideways and said, 'This is not fair.' dropping the spoon and leaning back.

'What isn't?' He asked, confused.

'This...! This whole thing. The dress, the car, the chocolates, this place, you... those eyes... Nothing is. I wanted to wait for a little longer before I could say it. But...'

I stopped mid-sentence inhaling deeply looking at his eyes and slowly onto his lips. He looked at mine and my mouth automatically opened like it was done waiting. In our minds, we were already kissing. The vibe was intense. He suddenly cleared his throat and said,

'Varna... I was just kidding when I challenged you. I don't want to force you to tell me something that you are not ready to tell. I understand.'

I leaned my head to the side and placed my hand on my chest, appreciating his gesture. I have been waiting for a special moment to tell him but I suddenly realized no moment or no words ever are going to do justice to the love I feel for him. But this, today would be a great start. As I was about to say something he stopped me and said, 'I have another surprise for you.' I looked at him doubtfully. He called out for the waiter and ordered the bill. He cheered me up with his silly jokes before the waiter could come. He eased the vibe for me. I offered to pay or at least split the bill but he strongly refused. He finished paying the bill and stood up, asking for my hand. I surrendered and walked with him. He took me towards the door where the sign said *No Entrance.*

I squeezed his hand and looked at him, questioningly but he just smiled. He started walking faster almost pulling me behind him. Him being a lot taller than me, I had to run behind him which made me laugh. He took us upstairs towards the door, probably to a further terrace, to which he had keys in his pocket. He opened the door and held it for me. As I entered the terrace, he closed the door behind us and took me to the parapet. I was awestruck by the view I saw. It was a tall building so we could see a huge part of Bangalore city in its full night glory. The beautiful tree tops covered most of the roads. The building lights and the red lights from the cars decorated the trees like flowers. The half-moon silently relaxed amidst the beautiful greyish night clouds and the cold breeze hitting my face now and then. It was just perfect.

I felt his hand slowly move from my shoulder to my waist. I looked sideways at his face and he pretended like nothing happened and was still enjoying the view, not daring to look at me. I stared at his face, smiling and admiring his beauty. Then I turned halfway towards him, held his collar and pulled him to face me. He was so surprised by the force with which I pulled, that his eyes went wide in shock. I set his collar back, lifted my heels to reach his face and put my arms around him. I looked down from his eyes to his lips, slowly bending towards them, and kissed him.

Initially, he was in shock but then once he got a hold of what was happening, he brought both his hands onto my waist and pulled me closer to him. Our lips felt like they are a perfect match for each other like a jigsaw puzzle. They played around comfortably. The kiss was gentle at first but then after a minute or so, it got so intense that when we released from the kiss, we both were slightly panting. The minute he left the hold, he moved a little backwards like he was staggering from the hangover that the kiss gave us. Then I finally blurted out, 'Subhash... I love you.' He looked at me, holding the parapet so he doesn't fall and sprinted back to me, holding my face in his palms and taking over my lips all over again. This time more passionately. Our bodies looked like we were merging into each other.

Chapter-17

It was the weekend and I woke up early, cleaned up the house, prepared breakfast and took a bath. Just as I was stepping out of the shower my phone started ringing. It was Subhash video calling me on WhatsApp. I cut the call and texted him that I just came out of the shower and would call him back later.

S: Nope. I have an emergency. Call me RIGHT NOW.

After our first kiss on that terrace three days ago, it felt like we had taken a few steps forward in our relationship. The first few days were all about the missed time, renewed friendship and longing for each other's company. But that one date changed everything. We started making video calls, complimenting each other's features and bodies. I believe I have developed a whole new sense that I was never aware of. We were exploring how beautifully we complemented each other. The kiss proved to be like a testimony to our chemistry. Our hearts and souls had enough, now it was the time for our bodies to play around and get to know each other. We didn't meet ever since that date but we have been desperate to do that again.

I quickly got dressed up, sat on the bed air drying my hair under the fan and called him.

'What is it, Subhash? Is everything okay? Don't tell me you are cancelling on us today.'

'No, of course not... Didn't you say you just came out of the shower? That was my emergency. Why did you have to get dressed so soon?'

I rolled my eyes and said, 'Yeah. This is all you are going to see today.' bending my head to cover my face with my hair.

'Well. It's still serving me. I could look at those curls all day. You know how much I love your hair right?' I sat back up and looked at him defeated.

'Are you ready to meet them?' I asked.

Akanksha and Aditya were coming to Bangalore today. They have been working so hard on their courses and Adi got a seat in CEPT Ahmedabad for further studies. Akanksha decided to stay back in Hyderabad and finish her Masters from here because she was not ready to leave her parents. So, it was their last few days together and I requested them to visit Bangalore so they can meet Subhash before he leaves for the US and Adi left for Ahmedabad.

Subhash knew it from the start, how important Akanksha was in my life. But he wasn't around by the time Adi became important too. I have been talking about them a lot and he was excited to meet them.

'Yes. Absolutely. I'll get the car and pick you guys up at 12. I know a great place for lunch. Is that okay?'

'Yes. Is it JW Marriott?' I asked teasingly.

'Hahaha, I wish... But no. That day the manager wasn't around so my friend could get us to the terrace. If we do that stunt again, the security will kick us out.'

'Hmm sounds like an adventure...' I said, teasing him more.

'You turned out to be such a daredevil Babe. It's so sexy!'

'Yeah... Let me throw a challenge at you. Today... in full daylight... outing with friends... you have to kiss me.'

'Whoa... That's tempting. Before you threw a challenge like that you should have known what kind of bad boy I am... I'm in.'

'Huh, I'm not going to make it that easy for you... You'll see!'

I said tempting him more. I was feeling pretty confident and hopeful that he would win the challenge. Just then the doorbell rang.

'Oh, I guess they are here. See you soon.' I cut the call and sprinted to the door. The second I opened the door; Adi pushed me aside and ran into the bedroom. Akanksha pulled me into a hug. 'What's with him?' I asked, confused.

'He needed to use the restroom but I don't trust the public ones so I made him wait until we came here.'

'Oh, poor guy. Going full Akanksha on him huh?'

'Yep... Dude, I love the place. The lighting is amazing and the balcony facing the road, Awww.' She said while walking around the house and ending up on the balcony. 'So, is this where you guys first met?'

'Yeah. He stood right there and waved at me.' I said showing her the spot I first saw Subhash. Just then Adi came and placed his arm on my shoulder and asked, 'Who stood right where?'

'Subhash... I was standing here, holding my coffee and then I saw him and ran downstairs and hugged him.'

'Awww that's romantic! So, tell us... How is he?' He asked in a concerned tone as we all went inside and sat on the dining table.

'He is more than anything I have ever imagined. He is considerate, loving, caring and romantic... And drop-dead gorgeous!'

'Wow. Lovely. I'm so happy for you Varna.' Akanksha said.

'He sounds great. I just truly wish he doesn't hurt you again.' Adi said.

I smiled at him understanding his concern.

I was ready and waiting for him, anxiously looking at the road, standing on the balcony. It was almost 12:05 pm when Subhash arrived. He got down the car and signalled to me if I wanted him upstairs. I said No as we were ready to go. As we walked downstairs, Subhash came to the gate and greeted us all. I introduced them to him. As we were proceeding to the restaurant, they all got comfortable and Adi and Subhash bonded over their love for sports and the amusement in teasing their girlfriends. I loved the vibe. I loved how easy it was for Subhash and for Akanksha and Adi to be around each other. It was irresistible to see him like that.

As we settled down and order food, Adi asked Subhash,

'So, Subhash... What is it that you are planning to do exactly after your MBA?'

'Well, I have a plan to start a cloud kitchen chain and expand it to all the major cities in South India. I already have a team helping me with the research here.'

'Oh, that's interesting. So, when you say cloud kitchen...?'

'There will not be any seating or any inflow of people but we will have a kitchen where we cook various cuisines and deliver via an app.'

'Oh, I have heard about this app called Swiggy... Is it something like that?'

'Yes. Like that. But this app is dedicated only to this restaurant. We will have a website and a hotline number too. I'm building a team with the best chefs in each cuisine.'

'Seems like there will be some risk too, right?' Akanksha asked.

'Yes. Any business has a few risks but if we assess what level of risks we will hit and how to avoid them, I think we will be just fine. It's all about how much initial groundwork you do. You need to know in and out of everything that's happening around you.'

I was just sitting there, staring at him and drooling over him. I didn't get to see this side of Subhash until then. I knew a little about his plans but the confidence he was displaying and the level of detail in which he was talking, the passion he felt while he spoke... it was all too attractive to someone like me. I have always been the same kind of ambitious person.

I came out of the trance and let myself out telling them that I needed to use the restroom. I texted him to come and meet me near the alley leading to the washroom. I hid in the small closet that was on the way to the restroom and when he passed by, I grabbed his hand and pulled him in. Before he could react or say anything, I kissed him with all the passion I was feeling. He joined in and felt me up, pulled me closer and kissed me more. Then I pushed him away, jumping out of the closet and said, 'Well... I'll see you back there. Oh, and by the way, I kissed you first, so I won.' He smiled with one side of his cheek, impressed.

When I went and sat at the table, they both started staring at me. I couldn't look them in the eye so I ignored them by immersing myself in the Menu card. A few seconds later, Subhash came in, wiping his hands. Akanksha and Adi fixed their gaze on us and didn't move. Subhash looked at them and said, 'What? I just went to the washroom.' I looked at him and winked from behind the menu card and he pinched my leg.

As we were almost finishing the meal, Adi said,

'So, Subhash. Your restaurant that we were discussing, will it be similar to the one like Gowtham's? In Vizag?' I widened my eyes, still looking at the food on my plate and Akanksha sat up straight and looked at Adi. He had no clue that I never told Subhash anything about the panic attacks, the mental breakdowns and the Vizag episode.

'Hmmm, not really. That's fusion food. Adding a desi touch to some Western food items.' Subhash answered but looked at Adi, confused and asked, 'I didn't know she told you about Gowtham's food court.' He added, thinking I told him what Subhash had told me when we were talking. Akanksha put her spoon on the plate and started staring at Adi so he would realize and stop talking but Adi didn't notice her and continued blabbering,

'Told me? Why will she tell me? I was there the whole time! Akshu was there too.' Adi said, thinking Subhash thought that I went to Vizag alone.

Subhash fell in complete confusion by now and the whole vibe around the table has changed into suspicious. He asked, 'What are you talking about?'

That was when it hit Adi that Subhash didn't know anything about our little Vizag trip. He looked at Akanksha and froze, who was clenching her teeth by now. I looked at Subhash for a second but couldn't look into his eyes so I just went back to eating. Subhash looked at the three of us and asked, 'Guys... What happened? How do you know Gowtham's?'

The circumstance was irreparable. Aditya, being the spoiler, took responsibility and started talking. But him being the stupid guy he was, started the story from the day Subhash left and I had my first panic attack. I left my spoon on the plate and leaned back, taking a deep breath. Subhash was shocked. He saw me reading the letter but he didn't stay till the point where I fainted.

Aditya told him all about the first panic attack and how I was grounded for a while, how I got low at studies, how I almost lost Akanksha and how I almost dated Adi. He went on and on about how the panic attacks kept repeating that whole year every time I thought about Subhash. Subhash covered his mouth with his hands, resting them on the table and kept listening intently. And then at that point, Akanksha took over. She told him how I revisited the letter and realized he was all that I ever wanted, how I convinced my parents and her to come along to Vizag.

Adi continued telling him about how we went to every fusion food joint to finally find Gowtham. He didn't leave out the part where Gowtham hit on me too. I did get a small laugh from Subhash for that. Adi continued and mentioned how we found Mahima and spoke to her too.

Even though I couldn't admit it to myself, Akanksha told Subhash that I chose Bangalore only in the hopes of seeing him, if he ever visits and then how we luckily found Aunty in the mall.

My head was spinning by now. The atmosphere became heavy and intense. I kept breathing heavily and making circles in my food. I couldn't imagine what Subhash must be feeling. There was almost 5 minutes of pin-drop silence at the table after the story ended. Subhash still had his hands covering his mouth. He was transfixed. I slowly turned completely towards him and put my hand on his shoulder and called him out.

He looked directly into my eyes with tears in his. He was biting his lower lip to gain the strength to say something. Our eyes and eyebrows were having a conversation of their own. Mine told him how much I love him and his told me that he couldn't believe what he just heard and he loves me back. He turned completely towards me, bent forward and kissed my cheek strongly. I dropped my head, letting him in and gently put the other arm around him too, bringing him into the hug. He scooted towards me, immersed his face into my neck and hugged me tightly with one arm on my back and placed the other on my head lovingly.

We were finally distracted by the waiter with the bill after a few minutes. The remaining part of the afternoon went by pretty quiet. We came out of the restaurant and Adi proposed to click pictures. When we finally reached my apartment, he stopped the car and looked at me. Akanksha intervened and said, 'Varna... Keys? We'll wait upstairs.' I handed over the keys to her, appreciating her level of understanding. After they left Subhash said,

'I'm so sorry Varna. To have put you through that. I had no clue.'

'No Subhash. It's not on you. I understand where you came from. It's all good now, okay? We are good. We are together. That's all that matters.' He kept staring at me, shaking his head.

'Urgh Varna... You are amazing. How did I get so lucky?'

'I should be the one saying that. I love you a lot, Subhash.'

'I love you more baby. Come here.' He said and hugged me again.

We remained in the car holding hands for ten more minutes and then I said I had to go. He nodded and hugged me again before I went out of the car. I waved at him and climbed the first flight of stairs when I suddenly felt my heart ache. It was tightening by the second and everything around me started to spin. The sweating came back and I tried to take deep breaths. This was more intense than the attacks I had been having in the last few days. I thought if I could pull myself together and go into the house, I wouldn't feel this because I would be distracted. So, I started walking upstairs but then the spinning started again and I collapsed on the stairs. Probably hearing me, Adi and Akanksha came running to my rescue. After settling me down, Akanksha handed me a glass of water and sat beside me with her hand on my shoulder. Adi was furious.

'Did that asshole do something to you again? I thought he was a good guy Varna. What the hell?'

'Adi, please. It's nothing. He hasn't done anything.'

'Then... what is this Varna? Is this the first time this happened after that date with Adi?' Akanksha asked with concern. When I shook my head a 'no' they both were shocked.

'When...? And why didn't you tell me? Is this before or after you came to Bangalore?'

'I had a mild attack the first day we met. I ignored it thinking I was probably tired because I hadn't slept much the previous night.'

'And?'

'A couple of times later... with minimum symptoms though.'

'And...?'

'I had one three days ago after our date night. It was intense too but I had it when I was almost about to sleep. I just closed my eyes and tried to fall asleep.'

'Oh my god Varna! What were you thinking not telling anyone about this? What if the breathlessness continued even in your sleep? Do you understand how threatening that sounds? I'm going to inform Uncle right away.' Akanksha took her phone out and started dialling.

'Dude... Nanna will panic and they'll ask me to move back to Hyderabad. Don't do that please.'

'Then what are you going to do about it?'

'I'll think about it and figure out triggers...'

'And...?' she asked demandingly.

'I'll tell Subhash.'

'Yes, You will. If you won't, then I will.'

I agreed with her and thought to myself *Shit I have to tell him now!*

Chapter - 18

Subhash's flight back to Pennsylvania was just a week ahead. I was in a constant depressive state imagining how much I was going to miss him. He wasn't doing great either. We kept meeting each other almost every day after my work but it didn't make the pain any less. I didn't get an opportunity to talk to him about my attacks too. I thought it was too gloomy and stressful to discuss that in the very little time we had together. But today, I decided we need to have one good night before he leaves because I wouldn't see him for another six months. So, I took half a day off and I texted him.

V: Subhash... What are you doing today?

S: Hey Babe. I went out for lunch with my school friend today. I'll come to the store at 5 30 pm.

V: No. Don't...

S: Why? Do you have plans? I'm here only for another week Varna...!

V: Relax... I have something else planned for us. Would you like to come to the house tonight?

S: What...!? It's been three weeks since I've been here but you never offered me to even come upstairs...!

V: Yeah, I know. It was mostly because it would be too dangerous to resist you in such closed quarters.

S: Well, I thought so too. I'm not sure if I can be a good boy if we had the entire place for ourselves. Varna... what are you planning?

V: Don't get any thoughts. I wanted to surprise you with a special date night, just like you did with JW Marriott, in my own way. What do you think?

S: Shall I start now?

V: Hahaha No. Dress up like you are going on a real date. Come by the house at 7 pm sharp. Text me when you reach the door.

S: I can't wait...! Will be there.

I went to the nearest grocery store and picked up vegetables and some items. Even though he enjoyed different cuisines, nothing hits the spot like homemade South Indian food for him. So, I decided to make my very famous *aloo fry*, *tomato pappu* and some papad for sides.

Later I swept, mopped and cleaned the apartment. I pulled the 5'x3' desk to the centre of the dining area and placed two chairs on either side of it. I got a pendant light, that I shopped with my dad, and fixed it to the light fixture above the table. I laid a tablecloth and arranged plates and food on the table. I put candles of different sizes all around the house on different platforms. I used some essential oils for a lavender-flavoured aroma. I closed the curtains and locked the balcony door. I looked around the house, appreciating how romantic a setting the house has turned into. I still had one hour before Subhash would come. So, I quickly jumped into the shower.

Even though my mom and dad always told me how great I looked in sarees, I haven't been very keen on wearing them often. But tonight, was special. I knew the love he had for the colour black. So, I decided to wear a black transparent saree with a gold border and a sleeveless black blouse.

I draped the saree intentionally a little below my belly button. I paired it with some gold terracotta earrings and left the neck empty. I blow-dried my hair and set it half to the front and half to the back so he can still see my back. I applied minimum makeup, nude lipstick and a black *bindi* to go with the saree. After I was done getting ready, I threw a flying kiss into the mirror. I still had 15 mins so I started lighting the candles. When I was almost done, I stood at the door and looked around to see what he would see when he entered. I felt pretty proud of myself. Just then I heard the bell ring. I ran into the bedroom to see myself in the mirror for one last time and then opened the main door.

There he was, looking stunning. Surprisingly he was wearing an all-black outfit too. The second I opened the door, he gasped and put his arm on his chest, scanning me from top to toe for several seconds and shook his head in disbelief.

'Varna... You... You look...' He kept sighing probably trying to find the right word. But I didn't let him finish. 'Come on in.' I said gently holding him. As he walked inside, I shut the door and turned around. I folded my hands and watched him slowly walk around the house, looking at every object, every room and every corner in detail and he said, 'Oh my god Varna... what is this place!? The smell, the aura, you... Am I dead? Am I in heaven?'

He turned sharply towards me when he heard me laugh at that comment. We locked eyes, I was still smiling but he wasn't. He looked like he was being hypnotized. I wanted to run and jump into his arms and kiss him like we were dying tomorrow. I inhaled sharply distracting myself from my thoughts. He walked towards me and put his right hand on my bare waist and slid it all the way to the back touching every inch of my skin and pulled me close, squeezing my breasts against his chest. He ran his fingers on my hand from the wrist to the shoulder and made circles around the edge of my neck. From there he slid them up from behind the ear and into my hair, all the while still maintaining eye contact. We then naturally came closer and kissed.

We kissed passionately for several moments until I had to push him away because I couldn't breathe. I took my phone and connected it to the Bluetooth speaker and started the playlist I carefully curated of 2000s Telugu romantic songs. He sat on the sofa and said, 'Wow. Varna... I'm highly impressed. No wonder you are an Arts student. This house, it is beautiful.'

I sat beside him and lifted his arm and wrapped it around my shoulder. He pulled me closer. We sat there discussing our favourite songs and movies of the 2000s for almost an hour. He gave me a list of Kannada classic movies to watch to get a better hold of the language. I stopped my playlist and played his favourite romantic song ever, as he mentioned, *Yeto Vellipoyndi Manasu* by SPB from the movie *Ninne Pelladata*. He stood up and asked for my hand. I frowned and doubtfully handed mine. He pulled me onto him with a thud and wrapped his hand around my waist and started dancing. I was taken aback by his excellent dance moves. He kept moving with one hand on my back and holding the other in his. He even rotated me. Our bodies moved in perfect harmony. As the song progressed further, he started singing the lyrics. I stopped moving and said, 'Wow. You can SING!'

'Oh yeah. I'm pretty good. I used to take Carnatic music classes in Hyderabad, remember?'

'Yeah right. It's coming back to me. I didn't know you sang this well. Your voice is beautiful.'

'Well, If you like, I can sing for you.'

'I would love it. Please...'

Then I sat there mesmerized by his voice and talent for half an hour. I had goosebumps when he sang songs from *Yeto Vellipoyindi Manasu* movie and dedicated to me. It was more special because it had history. I remember watching that movie when Subhash left and making a huge scene in the theatre. I remember how much I cried imagining myself in the characters of that film. After he was done, I went to him, grabbed his face and kissed his lips, marking my territory And also feeling extremely glad that I never have to feel like that again as I have him with me now.

'Varna... I have a gift for you.' He said while opened a small box with a thin gold chain and a small half-heart pendant which had the letter 'S' embossed on it. He pulled it out and asked me to turn. He ran his fingers along the back of my neck, pushing my hair to the front so he can see the lock of the chain. He put it on my neck and turned me towards him.

'It's perfect. Is this gold? Subhash... You didn't have to! And where's the other half?' Then he opened the top button of his shirt and showed the pendant he was wearing. That was the remaining half of the heart with the letter 'V' embossed on it.

'This is a reminder that wherever I am, however far I am, my heart belongs to you and yours to mine. Keep that part of me right here with you safely, okay?' he said and touched the part where the pendant landed on my chest. I smiled and nodded my head, looking at my pendant. He kissed my forehead gently and whispered, 'I love you... so much Varna. I wish I had the right words to express the vastness of my love but there aren't any.' I bent my head towards one side, put my hand on his cheek and said, 'I know...'

He then went ahead and took complete control of my body. He kissed my neck first, activating the most sensitive erogenous zone and I just gave in. He went around and kissed the back of my neck and my upper back which was exposed from the blouse and unstrapped the hooks. He came forward, started kissing my neck and slowly moved inch by inch. He kissed my chest as far as it was exposed and stopped where my blouse started. He kneeled and pushed my saree aside and kissed my belly button. He kept moving and exploring and landed on my love handles and bit me which made my body shiver. He then stood up and kissed my dried-up lips, now a little deeper. While our lips were kissing, our hands knew no limits. We raided each other's bodies and meanwhile, he somehow managed to remove the pin that was holding my saree securely on my shoulder. He moved away a little bit so that he can see. The saree slowly glided from my shoulder and dropped down. I smiled naughtily and lifted an eyebrow, pushing my hair towards the back. As the hooks of my blouse were already undone, I sensuously removed my blouse in slow moments, looking into his eyes and enjoying watching him go crazy. He opened his eyes and mouth wide and kept staring. I moved closer to him and ended up just an inch away from his body but didn't touch it. I started unbuttoning his shirt, maintaining the eye-lock. He put his hands on my back first and started moving them forward with slow moments, giving my body goosebumps. I was pleasantly surprised by what hit me. His body was a piece of art. As he was ogling my breasts, I unwrapped my saree and he promptly took care of his pants. He swiftly lifted me and took me to the bedroom and dropped me on my bed.

We lay on the bed, staring at the ceiling, reliving every second of the last 20 mins in our heads. The feeling was divine and ultimate. After resting for 5 full mins, he turned on his side, propped up on his elbow, hand supporting his head and started playing with my hair. He said,

'You looked delightful in that saree Varna!'

'Yeah. You proved it really well.' I said appreciatively and turned towards him. He kissed me on the cheek and went to the restroom. Meanwhile, I changed into a comfortable T-shirt and shorts.

When I was picking up the saree and the other clothes from the ground, I had another heavy panic attack. My breathing became difficult and my head started spinning rapidly. Before I could drop the clothes off on the bed and sit down, I completely collapsed on the floor. Just then Subhash came out of the washroom and ran towards me, yelling my name. Things started to blur and I heard noises with echoes. I pointed towards the dressing table drawer and Subhash quickly opened it and found my pills. I nodded weakly so he gave me the bottle and ran into the kitchen to get some water. I took a pill and pulled myself up to sit against the bedpost. Subhash sat beside me, pulled me into his arm and rested my head on his shoulder. He kept rubbing my arm gently until I slowly recovered and got back to normal. Once my breathing got normal, he asked, 'What just happened Varna?'

'A panic attack...'

'Oh, my god. Is this what Aditya was talking about? The year I left... You had these? Oh, my baby... What have I done to you...!?' He said and hugged me sadly. Then it struck me. It was because I still felt insecure about Subhash. I wanted him in my life desperately but anytime I have a great interaction with him, my mind panics that it might not last. As I recollected every time I had one of these, the clouds began to clear. I was in control of the situation.

'Subhash... I guess my mind still doesn't believe that you are here to stay. I have had some of the most beautiful memories in my life in the past few days. But it is too overwhelming for me. I'm feeling low that you are going to leave and it's reflecting now. I don't feel confident and secure that I have you in my life forever. I'm probably scared, what if this doesn't last... I'm really sorry.'

'Sorry? No! I left you in a very insensitive manner and I shouldn't have done that. I take complete responsibility for this Varna. It's on me. But what can I say that will assure you that this is our life now?'

'I don't know.'

'Nor do I baby... I don't know what to say that will get you better. But you listen to me. I'm going to try and make you feel loved, valued, wanted and respected as long as I live. I promise, look at me... I PROMISE.' He said, holding my hand in his and pressing it hard. I nodded and smiled.

'There is no end to this Varna. Believe me... I want to do life with you. I'm not going anywhere, ever! Even if I'm leaving, it'll not be the same as before. We can talk to each other every day and try to figure out a way to make this work.'

I hugged his arm into my chest and rested my head on his shoulder again. We sat there for a few minutes in silence, absorbing everything that just happened. And then he started talking again,

'I wanted to ask you something. I have my graduation ceremony in a month and I would love for you to be there. After all, I completely dedicate this achievement to you.'

I gasped and looked at him. At first, I thought he was just saying it but looking at him, I knew he meant it.

'Subhash... It's a big thing. I need to talk to my parents first. And no giving away credits, okay? It was your hard work.'

'Okay... Let me know when you talk to them. And now can we have that delicious-smelling food that you made? I'm starving.' I laughed standing up and helping him get up.

When it was finally time for him to leave, it became so difficult to contain my emotions. Tears kept rolling down like a dam gate just opened. His heart broke to see me like that. He hugged me and kissed the top of my head lovingly. I pressed my cheek against his chest, closed my eyes and found peace in the rhythm of his heartbeat. In that profound moment, with that hug, we embraced the memory of us in each other's arms, we embraced the fun times we had, the long rides we took on his bike, the sneaky kisses we had and the intense love we felt for each other.

Chapter - 19

2016

Two years later...

I boarded my early morning flight and anxiously looked out the window waiting for it to take-off. The last time I saw Subhash was nine months ago when he came to Hyderabad, looking for probable sites to start up his restaurant chain. And now it was time for the brand to spread to Vizag, which was always his dream. He had been in Vizag for the past week. He asked if I could spend the weekend there with him, so we could get some time away from our busy schedules and I obliged.

As the flight started to reverse, I decided to get some sleep and get rid of the puffiness in my face before I met him. As I drifted into sleep, the past two years started to flash in front of my eyes...

It took a lot of convincing for my parents to accept the trip to the University of Pennsylvania for his graduation. But when Subhash stepped up and called my dad to ask for permission, they couldn't say no. They felt it was okay when they knew his parents were coming too. It was a memorable trip. Uncle and I bonded over roasting Subhash and it was a lot of fun. We cheered and whistled when he took his graduate pin on stage and we celebrated his achievement at a fancy restaurant that evening.

He came back to Bangalore six months later, completely ready with his plans and proposals for his restaurant chain so he started right away. He partnered up with his school best friend and they went at it with full force. I tried to meet him every weekend but he was very occupied and distracted. I struggled with it because I couldn't concentrate on my work when I knew he was right around the corner but wouldn't meet. The panic attacks never happened again but I worried about them constantly. So, I quit my job and moved back to Hyderabad. Subhash did abide by his promise and never made me feel alone or unsafe ever. But it was also time for me start my career.

Subhash didn't take my leaving so well in the beginning and we had some hurdles because he wanted me around. But I had made up my mind.. I rented a small workshop and hired some fine workers and began executing my sketches. Initially, I collaborated with a few jewellery stores to sell my brand. But later, I started selling them directly online. Subhash helped me set up an Instagram account for my business and soon the brand blew up and we had orders from all over the state. We both became extremely busy with growing our businesses and with the very little time we had for each other, we tried to make the most of it. We missed each other terribly but we held on to each other strongly than ever.

A few months later, Subhash gave me the good news that they were making enough money to invest in the next city to spread their restaurant chain. The obvious choice was Hyderabad. He visited with his partner but stayed back for a couple of days after he left so he could spend time with me. That was when I invited him to the house and introduced him to Mom and Dad. My mom and he bonded so well that before he left, he said 'I love her! Can I just move in with you?' *Silly boy!* We did steal some passionate kisses in the car which left us wanting more. I still felt his hands pulling me closer and closer and kissing my face and neck and everything he could get his grip on...

I was woken up by a sudden turbulence on the flight, pulling me back to reality. The way my vision ended, all I could think of was his lips all over my face and his hands grabbing me so tightly that I couldn't breathe.

When I exited the airport, I looked around for him and was surprised to see him on a Royal Enfield, waving at me. He was wearing a pale blue semi-formal shirt with grey jeans and looked gorgeous. I sprinted up to him and hugged him.

'I missed you so much, baby.' He stated.

'I missed you more.' I declared, sitting on the rear seat and grabbing him from below the shoulders and resting my head on his back. He took me directly to the hotel he was staying in.

'Do you remember the bike?' He asked as we were in the elevator to go to his room.

'Of course, I do. We used to roam around in Bangalore on your bike.'

'Yeah. I rented it just yesterday so we can relive some of those memories.' He smiled naughtily at me.

'There are a lot of memories that need to be relived mister.' I said, winking at him. When the elevator door opened, we walked hastily towards his room. The moment we stepped inside, he shut the door and grabbed me. He pinned me to the wall and started kissing me. He worked his hands down my t-shirt and threw it on the bed, while I quickly unbuttoned his shirt. We kicked our pants away, all while still kissing. I pushed him away to take a breath and grabbed his hand and pulled him towards the bed. What the room saw next, was the most intense 15 minutes it probably had ever seen.

Later, I was resting on his shoulder and playing with his mildly grown chest hair. His arm was wrapped around me and he kept running his fingers on my arm gently. The experience was so relieving and therapeutic that we both fell asleep. After about half an hour I woke up and saw his sleeping face. My heart instantly melted away. It was so peaceful and calm. I went to the restroom without waking him up. By the time I took a shower and came out, he was standing near the window facing outside. He had a towel wrapped around his waist and nothing else. I silently stood there and appreciated what I was looking at when he turned back. He smiled broadly, walked towards me and kissed my forehead. 'I'll take a shower and come. And then I'll take you somewhere special. It's a surprise.' He said.

We got our breakfast packed and had it on the beach and made a little picnic out of it. We travelled for about 20 minutes from the beach and reached the top of a hill near Vizag. We could see the docks now and then at turnings. The surroundings were very secluded, calm and elegant. He stopped the bike in front of a huge villa and asked me to get down. I was completely mesmerized by its beauty. He went to the gate and grabbed the keys from his pocket and opened it.

'What are you doing? What is this place?' I asked, surprised.

He held my hand and took me in. It was a beautiful holiday house probably constructed in the 1990s. The furniture was antique and stunning. We walked through the hall and the rooms. He took me to the top floor into the largest bedroom. It had a huge teakwood bed with bed posts and a white transparent net with a royal vibe. Then he closed my eyes from behind and started walking me. When we reached a certain place, he moved his hands away. My mouth dropped to the floor and my eyes were wide open in surprise. I didn't see that coming and I did not believe what I was looking at.

It was a huge 10'X10' balcony with wooden flooring facing the sea. My eyes were filled with the blues of the water. I couldn't move or say a word but just stared at the view. He wrapped both his arms around my neck and whispered into my ears, 'This is yours if you want it.' I frowned in confusion and turned to face him. 'What do you mean?'

'This belongs to my friend's grandfather and he was planning to sell it. When I first looked at the house and this view... I knew you would love it. So, I put an offer on the house. If you are interested and if you like it, I want to gift it to you.' I blurted out a laugh but his expression didn't change.

'You are not joking? Is this for real?'

'Absolutely. I'm making good money now. And wherever we decide to settle, either in Hyderabad or in Bangalore, I would love for us to have this as a holiday home. We can maybe put it on Airbnb and use it when we are here.'

'Subhash... This place... is astounding.'

'Is that yes?'

'I don't know! But this is too much. I would like to pitch in too. Let's share the burden. Maybe then I can consider it?'

'Hahaha Varna. We can do that when we buy a house that we live in. This is purely a gift from your loving to-be husband.'

I shook my head in disbelief and turned back towards the sea. I took a deep breath and leaned my head against his chest. Then I remembered the dream I had when I first fell in love with him.

I just came home from my morning jog and started making filter coffee. I served it in two mugs with our names on them, a gift from our sons for our anniversary. I took the coffee mugs into the balcony where he was just finishing his yoga routine. The balcony was almost like a room, 10'X10' with a beautiful view overlooking the beach. As I walked in, he came and sat on the wicker chair on one side of the balcony and I took the other. He took his mug and read the headlines of the newspaper, giving me general news updates. Just then our grandchild came running into the balcony wishing us Good Morning and sat in my lap. I kissed and hugged him while his mom came in with a tray carrying his milk and tea for her and her husband, my son. We all sat together and were drinking our beverages when my other son came home from his morning run. They were identical twins. He brought his protein shake into the balcony and sat with us. My grandson immediately dropped down from my lap and went and sat with my second son. After a little while we all dispersed and became busy with our schedules. My husband and my second son, who was going to take over our business, were discussing different ideas for business growth. I got freshened up and started for my work in my car and on the way, I dropped my grandson near the bus stop where his school bus would come and pick him up. I looked back at the bungalow. It was a beautiful two-storeyed individual house with lots of open spaces and a spacious garden. There he was, Subhash, looking at me from the balcony. When I smiled and waved at him, he threw a flying kiss and waved back.

I could visualize everything right there. The balcony, the view, the wicker furniture and the old me and Subhash. I closed my eyes and I could hear my future sons talking and my sweet little grandson's giggles. I laughed to myself. I walked towards the parapet and looked at the road and saw my old self looking back to the balcony. And the old Subhash right beside me, waving at me with so much love. I could see it all. I was more than eager to build this life for us. As I was smiling to myself, completely lost in my thoughts, Subhash came closer and wrapped his arms around my waist and rested his chin on my shoulder and said,

'What is it sweetheart? What are you thinking?'

I took a deep breath, put my palm on his cheek and said, '...Let's do this.'

He stood up straight and almost did a little dance. He pulled me into his hug and started singing and dancing around on that balcony. I couldn't help but laugh at his excitement and happiness. When we were finally done dancing and about to leave, I looked back at the view and the balcony and smiled with my heart knowing I was about to live my dream.

www.ingramcontent.com/pod-product-compliance
Lightning Source LLC
LaVergne TN
LVHW041918070526
838199LV00051BA/2660